brio® devotional series

want more? Joy™

by jeanette hanscome

TYNDALE

Tyndale House Publishers, Inc.
Carol Stream, Illinois

Want More? Joy

Copyright © 2006 by Focus on the Family.

A focus on the family book published by
Tyndale House Publishers, Carol Stream, Illinois 60188

TYNDALE is a registered trademark of Tyndale House Publishers, Inc. Tyndale's quill logo is a trademark of
Tyndale House Publishers, Inc.

Ediors: Lissa Halls Johnson, Liz Duckworth
Cover design and cover photo: Sally Leatherman
Interior design: Jeff lane, Smith/Lanne Associates
Interior photography:
Sarah Bolser: 11, 13, 14, 15, 17, 19, 21, 98, 99, 100, 101, 102, 104, 105, 106, 109, 110, 120, 124, 125, 127,
129, 131, 132, 143, 144, 146, 147, 151, 154, 156
Melinda Lane: 27, 45, 47, 48, 49, 51, 65, 70, 77, 78, 79, 81, 96, 111, 112, 114, 139, 142
Matti Stevenson: 29, 40, 41, 43, 44, 56, 58, 69, 71, 72, 116, 119, 128, 137, 148, 152
Andrea Flanagan Photography: 138, 140

Printed in Thailand
1 2 3 4 5 6 7 8 9 / 10 09 08 07 06

ISBN-10: 1-58997-231-7
ISBN-13: 978-1-58997-231-5

dedication

To the ladies in my critique group:
Diane, Peggy, Kaydie, and Maridy

Thanks for listening to all my bad first drafts, helping me search for scriptures, encouraging me, and especially praying for me. What would we do without each other?

Contents

God Told Me To

the Lord had filled them with joy

"Sing joyfully to the LORD, you righteous; it is fitting for the upright to praise him. . . . Sing to him a new song; play skillfully and shout for joy." (Psalm 33:1,3)

When God's people finally got permission to rebuild the temple in Jerusalem after their captivity in Babylon, they celebrated for seven days, "because the Lord had filled them with joy" (Ezra 6:22).

When Israel grieved over Nehemiah's reading of the Law, he told them to stop crying and have a celebration, reminding them, "The joy of the Lord is your strength" (Nehemiah 8:10).

After giving birth to the child she had ached and prayed for, Hannah said, "My heart rejoices in the Lord" (1 Samuel 2:1) even as she prepared to leave her son to be raised in the temple.

A couple of generations later, as the men of Israel marched into Jerusalem with the Ark of the Covenant, David danced with such uninhibited excitement that his wife rebuked him.

Several times God Himself called for His people to set aside time for rejoicing.

The book of Psalms is filled with proclamations of joy:

"But may all who seek you rejoice and be glad in you; may those who love your salvation always say, 'The Lord be exalted!'" (Psalm 40:16).

"Those who look to him are radiant" (Psalm 34:5).

"Shout with joy to God, all the earth!" (Psalm 66:1).

During Jesus' last days with His disciples, He encouraged them that by seeking God for everything, their joy would be complete (see John 16:24).

Throughout the Old and New Testament, men and women of God wept, leapt, and sang with joy. They certainly didn't have easy, stress-free lives, but when they recognized God's goodness to them, they couldn't help but overflow with rejoicing and praise.

All of this shows me that God wants me to be joyful.

In her wonderful book Taking Up Your Cross: The Incredible Gain of the Crucified Life, Tricia McCary Rhodes writes, "God did not make man for duty or drudgery or even ordinariness. He created Him for joy."[1] She describes Christian joy this way: "Joy is our jubilant response to the presence of the living God who has made His home within our souls."[2]

So if joy is something God wants for me, and supposedly a response to His presence in my life, then why doesn't it flow out more naturally? Why am I not joyful all the time?

Maybe it's because I confuse joy with happiness. I looked both words up in the dictionary and found almost identical definitions, but I've learned from life that they're two different things.

Happiness seems to be dependent on my circumstances. I see God answering prayers; I don't have any major problems to worry about, so I'm happy.

Joy comes from a deeper place—a corner of

rejoice

radiant

joy

flow

confuse

rejoice

radiant

joy

flow

confuse

my soul that trusts in God's faithfulness and love and refuses to let the downs of life keep me from smiling, laughing and praising Him.

Have you ever seen photos of families from the 1800s? Judging from the expressions on the faces of the men, women, and children, you'd think they'd never had a happy day. God could have easily called us to be as solemn and dull as those old black-and-whites—no smiles, color, or evidence of future fun. After all, He is holy and perfect; we aren't.

All creation fell because of sinful humans who, from birth, can't follow the rules. He knows the ugliness of each of our hearts. He sent His Son to die for us; we accept His free gift and go right on sinning. We don't deserve to enjoy anything.

Yet our gracious, loving God allows us to experience joy and fills us with a natural desire for it. Through His Word He calls us to be a joyful people—children that radiate His light.

Psalm 33:4 only begins to list the reasons I have for joy. In a world full of lies and deception, "the Word of the Lord is right and true." When people let me down, "he is faithful in all he does."

Verses 6-9 reveal that I serve the God who created the universe and holds the world in order, even when it seems out of control.

I can celebrate the joy of my salvation, God's constant watch over me, and so much more.

As a daughter of God, I have the Source of joy at my side at all times, ready to fill me, equipping me to draw others to His goodness on the best days and on the worst.

Who Owns You?

What makes
something
valuable?

Rumor says Napoleon's toothbrush sold for two million dollars. Who would pay two million dollars for a dirty old toothbrush? Or thousands for a fake pearl necklace that belonged to a U.S. President's wife? Think about all the dresses that are worn only once by celebrities before being auctioned off for thousands. It's insane!

I have some fake beads of my grandmother's. They're not worth much to anyone else, but to me they are priceless. So are her books and my grandpa's little cardboard-framed picture of Jesus.

What makes something valuable? Often it's who owned it, not the item's rare beauty or exceptional quality.

Just for fun, browse through your house to find something that is valuable to you because it belonged to a precious grandparent, sibling, friend, or someone else you really care about. Maybe it's an old, beat-up children's book or a bracelet that cost only a few dollars.

Once you find that piece of jewelry, stuffed animal, book, piece of crystal, or clothing item, write a description worthy of it. Explain why it's so valuable to you and how you would feel if it was destroyed.

. . . .

. . . .

. . . .

. . . .

. . . .

. . . .

. . . .

Read what you wrote out loud and think how this could be a reminder of your value to God. Like that treasure of yours, you are precious because of your Owner.

The Father of the universe paid a high price for you as a child of God, and He won't give you up no matter how much money anyone offers Him. You are too precious to Him. He would never dream of packing you away with a box of old junk or selling you at a garage sale. You are His valuable joy, no matter what you look like, who your friends are, where you live, or how many limitations you have. What others say about you, think about you, or how they treat you doesn't change how God treasures you.

When I really absorb the knowledge of this value, I can't help but feel better about myself. The Creator of the universe loves me, just as I am! I can walk with more confidence. My mood soars. I have more self-respect. I don't need to give in to peer pressure or do dumb things to impress my friends because I'd rather please the One who really cares about me!

I wish I could say I feel confident all the time. When it comes to my typical frame of mind, the scenario in the paragraph above is more the exception than the rule. Honestly, it's extremely difficult for me to let my incredible value in Christ infiltrate my life. More often, I let negative input—like the insensitive words of others, even if they hurt me 10 years ago—scream louder than the opinion of the Lord who loved me enough to die a painful death in my place. When I hear a mean comment or face rejection, even a quick reminder that God approves of me, no matter what, doesn't make the pain or disappointment go away.

It's also much easier to receive my value from things I can touch and see, attempting to

million

pearl

insane

old

value

million

pearl

insane

old

value

impress people with my gifts and accomplishments, making sure that I have the right friends. But my high position in the eyes of an invisible God? It's harder to grab hold of that.

The things of this world that make me feel good—friends, talent, physical appearance—are great while they last, but they have this terrible tendency to let me down when I least expect it. They are frighteningly temporary. The value that I have in Christ never ends.

Still, I know that God wants me to grasp my high value, a value that I can have only through His Son. So I surround myself with reminders and run to them as often as I need to—daily, hourly, every minute if I'm having a particularly bad day. I hang quotes on my wall, read books about my significance in Christ, and listen to friends who are quick to remind me where my true worth lies. Most importantly, I am trying to listen more to what God has to say to me through His Word.

So, let this thought carry you through the day. When life causes you to forget your worth—when you feel rejected, passed over, or like a hopeless failure—stop and grab onto a reminder that the King of the universe owns you. Surround yourself with as many reminders as possible. Line your walls with them like you do your favorite posters.

Because of Who owns you, you are priceless and precious.

a special prayer

joy

Heavenly Father, sometimes I feel so worthless. Yet, the fact that I belong to You gives me eternal value. Why do I so often forget? Help me today to rejoice in my true worth. Thank You for purchasing me, and for loving me simply because I am Yours. Amen.

questions:

List the things that make you feel the most valuable.

. . . .
. . . .
. . . .
. . . .

How does popularity or having the acceptance of others affect your feelings of worth?

. . . .
. . . .
. . . .

Write about a time when someone's cruelty crushed your sense of worth, or when you failed at something you're usually good at.

. . . .
. . . .
. . . .
. . . .
. . . .

If you haven't recovered from the blow yet, write a prayer asking God to help you accept and cling to your value in His eyes.

. . . .
. . . .
. . . .
. . . .

joy

Which Bible verses remind you of your value in Christ?

. . . .
. . . .
. . . .
. . . .

dig deeper

What do the following Scriptures reveal about your value in God's eyes?

Genesis 1:24-31 . . . .
. . . .
. . . .

John 17:20-24 . . . .
. . . .
. . . .

Ephesians 1:4-6 . . . .
. . . .
. . . .

1 Peter 1:3-5

. . . .
. . . .
. . . .

1 Peter 1:18-19

. . . .
. . . .
. . . .

prayer challenge:

Ask God to help you place the same value on others as He places on you.

The Reject Bin

A t a popular candy factory jelly beans are meticulously sorted. Only those that arrive at the end of the line with a perfect shape, size, texture, and gloss qualify for a package bearing the company logo. The rest are considered flops and dropped into the reject bin.

Since the bin contains more than a million beans that still taste fine—even if they are ugly—the imperfect candies are dumped into big bags and sold in the factory gift shop. Instead of being artfully displayed on racks or filling pretty jars, the bags are heaped on a table and sold dirt cheap.

The ironic thing is that these cast-off candies are hot sellers. Every other person in the gift shop has a bag—or several bags—of funny-looking jelly beans.

Maybe I appreciate these yummy undesirables because I started out as a flop, destined for the reject bin. At least that's the way some saw me. When I was a baby, Mom

struggled to find out exactly what was wrong

noticed that I squinted all the time and turned my head away from bright light. While other infants stared at their moms with awe, I wouldn't keep eye contact with my parents.

It took eye doctors eight years to find out that I had a rare vision problem called Achromatopsia, a condition that leaves me without cone cells in my eyes. Cone cells are needed for filtering out bright light, distinguishing color, and seeing details.

While my parents waited and struggled to find out exactly what was wrong with my eyes, and eventually my sister Sherry's eyes, they heard all kinds of discouraging comments from doctors and teachers.

"Stop treating your daughter like she's normal. She isn't."

"Maybe Jeanette can't learn colors because she just isn't smart."

"Next year we'll probably start teaching her Braille and get her ready to transfer to a school for the blind."

"Most likely, your daughter won't go to college."

Even after transferring to a school district that had a great program for visually impaired kids and finding an excellent eye doctor who insisted that Sherry and I be treated as normal, I still found myself feeling like a dud sometimes. I wasn't exactly a top pick for sports teams. My dark glasses, constant blinking, odd reading style (with the page almost touching my nose) made me an easy target for teasing. Busy teachers didn't appreciate the extra help I needed.

It didn't help that nobody ever made fun of my sister Sherry. What was so special about her? Worse yet, what was wrong with me? Maybe those doctors and teachers were right. I wasn't normal. I was a flop.

In high school I discovered drama and public speaking. My classmates seemed to forget about my weirdness and appreciate my abilities. But the damage had already been done. Behind my good acting skills, I still felt like a defective product.

One thing helped. Mom and Dad shared stories from my early years. I guess I'd proven those "experts" wrong. What would they say if they found out that their dud actually graduated from a regular high school, was involved in normal activities, finished college, and enjoyed a rich life?

So when those moments of insecurity come—and they still do—I look at how God turned those dismal predictions around. In His eyes I am not flawed; I turned out exactly as planned. Sure, He gave me limitations, but He also gave me strengths. I don't hide defects behind my talents. Instead, they are proof that I am more than "that girl with the vision problem." The world may not have expected a lot from a kid who was legally blind, but my Creator had great plans for her.

I love to read about God turning "rejects" into amazing tools for His glory. Look at the way Jesus reached out to them. In a society where anyone with a disability was considered cursed by God, Jesus saw a blind man and told His disciples, "This happened so that the work of God might be displayed in his life" (see John 9:1-3). Instead of pushing him away as the rest of the crowd did, Jesus healed the man!

He chose men and women with social limitations—tax collectors, women, and dirty fishermen—to share in His ministry and spread the gospel.

God is not limited by our limitations. In fact, they provide greater opportunities for Him to show the truth in 2 Corinthians 12:9, "my power is made perfect in weakness."

When I think of my life this way, I not only stop seeing myself as flawed, I actually thank God for my low vision that is entirely absent of color, and any other weaknesses that leave me dependant on Him and His ability to do the unexpected.

gloss

flop

reject

defect

perfect

gloss

flop

reject

defect

a special prayer   *joy*

God, living in a world that demands and praises perfection makes it really hard to accept my "flaws." I thank You for the plans You have for me, plans that go far beyond the expectations of others. Thank You that, in Your eyes, I am a perfect creation, Your masterpiece.

questions:

What limitations (physical, social, developmental, etc.) do you fear might hold you back in the future? . . . .
. . . .
. . . .

How has God allowed you to excel beyond your expectations or the expectations of others? . . . .
. . . .
. . . .
. . . .

What are your greatest strengths? . . . .
. . . .
. . . .
. . . .

How has God used your limitations for good? . . . .
. . . .
. . . .

Which biblical hero do you admire most and why? . . . .
. . . .
. . . .

joy

What were his or her weaknesses? . . . .

. . . .

. . . .

How did God use this person despite his or her handicap, background, or character

flaws? . . . .

. . . .

. . . .

dig deeper

Read John 9:1-11

How might the blind man's life have been different if he'd been born during

modern times? . . . .

. . . .

. . . .

How do you think his life changed after Jesus healed him? . . . .

. . . .

. . . .

Read 2 Kings 5:1-15.

While Naaman was a powerful man, why would he have been considered a

"reject"? . . . .

. . . .

. . . .

How did God use Naaman's weakness for His purpose? . . . .

. . . .

. . . .

Balance?

"A large mocha, please," Dana ordered at the Coffee Cavern. She covered a yawn. "With an extra shot of espresso." She turned to her friend Madelyn. "I should have made that two extra shots."

"If you keep living on caffeine, you're going to turn into a coffee bean. I'm surprised your eyes haven't turned brown," Madelyn said, then ordered a caramel latte.

While waiting for the coffees, Dana pulled out the Palm Pilot that Dad had given her for Christmas. She reviewed her schedule for the day.

7:50 - school

12:15 - debate team meeting

3:00-5:30 - baby-sit Bradley beasts/kids

5:45-7:15 - dinner and homework

7:30-9:00 - worship band practice

Madelyn peeked over Dana's shoulder. "You have to remind yourself to go to school?"

"Hey, I'm a busy girl." She shut down the Palm Pilot and stuck it into her backpack. "You should see tomorrow's schedule. I start tutoring at the Boys and Girls Club."

"Dana!" Madelyn put her hands on her hips. "You said . . . "

"I changed my mind. If I want to get into an Ivy League college, I need more community service experience."

"God isn't going to wipe your name from His book if Princeton turns you down." Madelyn grabbed both coffees off the counter and handed Dana's to her.

"But my family might." Dana sipped her coffee, following Madelyn to her car. "Oh no, I forgot! I have a trig test today. I didn't study."

"You'll still get an A." Madelyn stopped at her car. "Hey, let's go see the new Leonardo DiCaprio movie this Saturday."

Dana shook her head. "I can't. I have to work on my term paper."

Madelyn opened the car door. Both girls hopped in. Madelyn stuck her coffee into a cup holder and held out her hand. "Give me that Palm Pilot. Come on, hand it over."

Dana fished it out of her backpack.

Madelyn pulled up Dana's

You have to remind yourself to go to school?

schedule, clicking from one day to the next. "Baby-sitting, tutoring, homework, debate team, term paper, worship team, student council. What about fun? When do you just hang out and do nothing? When do you spend time with God?"

Dana slouched in her seat. "What exactly is hanging out and doing nothing?" And spending time with God? She hadn't had a quiet time in weeks. The worst part was, she never enjoyed anything anymore. Even activities that had once been fun, like singing with the youth group worship band, felt like chores. Now she was forgetting things, like tests. She kept telling herself that life would slow down soon—after the big debate tournament, after her SAT prep class. But she always managed to fill the gap with something new.

"I guess I've become kind of a poster girl for over-achievement, huh?"

"You could say that." Madelyn handed the Palm Pilot back to Dana. "If you don't cut some things out, you're going to burn out."

"But what can I drop?" Dana sighed and took another sip of coffee. "Okay, I'll drop the tutoring."

"And?"

Dana thought. "I'll try to fit some fun in."

"Believe me, you'll be a much happier person, not to mention a nicer friend to be around."

"What do you mean, 'nicer'? It's not like

yawn

busy

debate

fun

nothing

yawn

busy

debate

fun

nothing

I've turned mean."

Madelyn looked at Dana. "Well, let's just say you wouldn't win any 'sweetest girl in school' awards these days."

Dana moaned. "Sorry. Maybe that movie would be a good idea."

It's pretty easy to get into a situation like Dana's, overwhelmed by a jam-packed schedule. Face it. The demands of school, activities, and parents are bad enough. Add a part-time job, volunteer work, or serving at church, and life can feel like an overstuffed backpack. It's twice as bad if you feel pressure to achieve certain standards—getting into a top college, maintaining straight As.

I have found myself in Dana's situation many times. I pack my day planner to capacity until someone points out, "You are too overloaded." Until then, I walk through life with tunnel vision, half asleep, forgetting things even if I make notes to myself. What I once excelled at I suddenly do half as well. Like Dana, I'm too tired to enjoy my favorite activities. Usually it's the important things that get pushed off my plate— my family, time with friends, God. Worst of all, I turn into my own evil twin, grouchy and snapping at everyone who gets in my way.

The writer of Ecclesiastes said, "I commend the enjoyment of life" (Ecclesiastes 8:15). That's pretty hard to do when each moment is sucked up into the busyness vacuum. So I'm learning to incorporate balance—time for work, play, family, friends, and my God—and to know when to say no. Life is so much better when I actually have time to enjoy it.

a special prayer

Father, there are so many things that I want to do, so many goals to reach. But what good is any of it if I burn out before I get there? Show me what is important and what I should give up. Help me to prioritize according to Your agenda. Amen.

questions:

Think about your typical week. How much time is devoted to the following:

School . . . .

Homework and studying . . . .

Extracurricular activities . . . .

Church attendance . . . .

Church-related activities or service . . . .

Part-time job (baby-sitting counts) . . . .

Volunteer work or community service . . . .

How much time do you spend:

Praying and reading your Bible; being alone with God? . . . .

Sleeping . . . .

Hanging out with friends . . . .

Hanging out with your family . . . .

Pursuing hobbies . . . .

Relaxing and doing nothing (watching TV or movies, lying in bed listening to music, and sleeping in count here) . . . .

In what area of life (school, church events, extracurricular activities) do you most often find yourself overcommitted? . . . .

. . . .

. . . .

How does this affect other important areas of your life? . . . .
. . . .
. . . .
. . . .

How much of your packed schedule is your choice? . . . .
. . . .

What can you cut back on? . . . .
. . . .
. . . .

What is usually the first signal that you are overloaded? . . . .
. . . .

Write a prayer asking God to help you prioritize and to see the rewards that come when you do. . . . .
. . . .
. . . .
. . . .
. . . .
. . . .

dig deeper

Read Mark 6:30-32.
Why did Jesus' disciples need to get away? . . . .
. . . .

What does this passage tell you about Jesus and the value that He places on rest? . . . .
. . . .
. . . .

I Thought You Were Different

fought an
urge to
laugh out
loud

Jacqueline was outgoing, smart, and nice to everybody. But the other kids in our drama class noticed only that she needed makeup but never wore it, that her clothes were out of style, and she had bad taste in music.

"Check out her outfit," Allie whispered to Rachel as Jacqueline finished performing a scene. "Wal-Mart must have had a sale in the old lady department."

Rachel imitated a whiney child. "I want a shirt like that. And Allie, will you please do my hair like hers? P-lease?"

Rachel and Allie laughed so hard that they both snorted. Jacqueline's hairstyle basically had no style.

I had a long list of reasons to stick up for Jacqueline. She had been friendly to me since the first day of school, even though she was a senior and I was only a freshman. Anytime I performed in class, and when I got a part in the school play, she showered me with compliments. Okay, she could be annoying and weird, but did that mean she deserved to get torn to shreds?

I guess the pressure to fit in was too much. Instead of defending Jacqueline, I fought an urge to laugh out loud along with Allie and Rachel. Before I knew it, I had thrown in a one-liner about Jacqueline's weight.

"You're cruel," Allie smirked.

The constriction around my heart told me that Allie was right, even if she wasn't sincere. But for some insane reason, it felt good to side with the popular girls for a change, to dish out the put-downs instead of receiving them.

The fun ended abruptly when Jacqueline turned to face us.

nice

taste

cruel

hate

smart

nice

taste

cruel

hate

She had heard every cruel word. I looked away when she stared right at me, like she wanted to cry out, "You too? I thought you were different."

The next day I ran into Jacqueline's sister, Karri, while waiting in line for lunch. I had known Karri since fourth grade. She would hate me if she found out what I did. My stomach turned a double somersault.

"I am so mad today." Karri scowled. "Jacqueline broke down crying last night. She said a bunch of girls in drama class were making fun of her."

I waited for Karri to add, "Jacqueline said you were in on it too," and really lay into me. Instead, she went on about how sweet and accepting Jacqueline was, how knowing that Jacqueline would never hurt a living soul made her even angrier. My cheeks burned with shame.

As far as I knew, Jacqueline never mentioned my name as she cried to her family. It didn't matter. Just knowing that I helped cause her tears—that I inflicted the same pain on her that I had felt so many times—was enough to break me. Why had impressing those girls been so important? It sure wasn't worth the guilt I felt now.

I could still kick myself for not grabbing the first opportunity to apologize to Jacqueline and her sister. Instead, I took the easy way out. I made an extra effort to be nice to Jacqueline and vowed to never be so shallow and mean again. But I never forgot what I did.

Even now, if I catch myself putting someone down, Jacqueline's devastated face often flashes through my mind. "I thought you were different," a voice confronts.

That's usually enough to get my attention. But not always. Sometimes I'm disappointed at how quickly I forget the lesson that my awful words about Jacqueline taught me.

Verses like Ephesians 5:1-2 have stopped me in my tracks again and again: "Be imitators of God, therefore, as dearly loved children and live a life of love, just as Christ loved us."

What do I gain if I tear apart an innocent victim? Does it make me happy? No! Whether I get caught or not, I feel awful inside.

It's much better to be known as a compassionate person than as one who makes people feel bad about who they are. The "popular" crowd may not be too impressed with me. But in the end, I have more genuine friends and fewer regrets. And what could be better than knowing that I am living as an imitator of God and loving as Christ loves?

As much as I wish I could go back and relive that afternoon in drama class, I thank God for the wake-up call. Jacqueline's face is immortalized in my mental file box. It is a reminder that a willingness to stand as an example of Christ's loving acceptance is far greater than looking into eyes that silently cry out, "I thought you were different."

a special prayer

joy

Father, each person is precious to You. Who am I to put anyone down—to say, "You aren't good enough"? Forgive me for those times when I put my pride above the feelings of one of Your children. Thank You for showing me the rewards of living a life of love. Amen.

questions:

After reading the description of a "child of light" in Ephesians 4:29—5:2, give some examples of when your life reflected this passage.

. . . .

. . . .

When haven't you? . . . .

. . . .

In what areas could you use some work? . . . .

. . . .

What benefits have you found in being kind to "outcasts"? . . . .

. . . .

How do you feel when you know you have hurt someone? Compare that to how it feels to show Christ-like love. . . . .

. . . .

. . . .

. . . .

How far are you willing to go to be accepted by the "right crowd"? . . . .

. . . .

. . . .

Think about some of the most popular kids at school. Now, what about those who aren't so well liked? How do you think these kids earned their status or lack of status? Who would you honestly rather spend time with? Why? . . . .

. . . .

. . . .

. . . .

What makes you happiest: **saying negative things about** people or building others up? . . . .

. . . .

dig deeper

Read Romans 15:5-7. List some people you have a hard time accepting and explain why. . . . .

. . . .

. . . .

Now list faults that God has accepted in you. . . . .

. . . .

. . . .

How can you reach out to one person on your list this week? . . . .

. . . .

. . . .

Read Romans 12:16. Why do you think it is so difficult to associate with those of "low position"? . . . .

. . . .

. . . .

How difficult is it for you? . . . .

. . . .

In Danger of Failing

I'd kept my secret for three long days. My prayers that the Rapture would take place before I broke the news to Mom and Dad had gone unanswered. How would I ever find the words? Now I knew why so many kids dreaded progress report time.

Most of my teachers didn't bother giving progress reports to A students, or even those with a C average or better. Why waste the paper when they could save those special gems for scholars that truly deserved them? This particular quarter I didn't get one progress report; I got three. Three incriminating "Homework missing," "Low test scores" progress reports.

I missed a test—okay, three tests

I sat in my bedroom staring at those awful half-sheets, each with an ugly black check marking the "In danger of failing" box. If I didn't turn them in tomorrow, I would lose points I couldn't afford to lose.

If I'd received the progress reports because I didn't understand how to find the surface area of a rectangular prism, or the proper use of a semicolon, or why the U.S. entered WWII, maybe I wouldn't have dreaded facing my parents so much. Instead, my grades revealed a terrible truth: Many of my answers to school-related questions had been lies.

"Did you do your homework?"

"Yes." The easy stuff that is. They didn't ask if I finished it.

"Do you have any tests to study for?"

"No." Okay, I do, but I don't need to study for it.

I guess I'd been too busy hanging out at the mall with my friend Tina and watching reruns of favorite sitcoms to work out equations, memorize dates, and read boring short stories. Obviously I never expected losing 10 points here and there would catch up with me. But now, here I sat, "in danger of failing."

I gathered the courage to approach Mom and Dad and thought up every excuse imaginable.

"Remember that week when I was sick? I don't think the teachers added in my makeup work."

"I missed a test—okay, three tests."

"See, Mr. Smith hates me!"

All I came up with were more lies to hide the many I'd already told my parents that quarter.

Here's the condensed version: I confessed. Mom and Dad went ballistic and grounded me from every TV show that had kept me from doing homework. They told me that I could see Tina only on weekends, and insisted on weekly progress reports from my teachers.

One more thing happened. The sick feeling in my stomach—the guilt, the dread—disappeared. I had received my consequences, could live through them, and move on. Mom and Dad were mad, but they still loved me. The memory of carrying home three progress reports motivated me to never let my grades slip again.

Since then I've had to confess plenty of other mistakes. Often, as with the progress reports, my sins had to catch up with me first.

"I looked through that book you're been

secret

broke

dreaded

test

numb

secret

broke

dreaded

test

numb

hiding in your room. It may have teen characters in it, but it's not for teens."

"How long were you on the phone long distance?"

"You girls had a party while we were gone, didn't you?"

In each case, I started out making excuses, but in the end saw it was best to confess, face the consequences, and try not to do it again.

I'm actually glad God never allowed me to get away with much. If I broke a rule, Mom, Dad, or a teacher usually found out. If I rebelled in secret, guilt ate away at me until I stopped. I may have fun breaking rules or avoiding responsibility for a while—or at least think I'm having fun—but praise God that it doesn't last.

When King David committed his string of sins with Bathsheba, he wasn't just "in danger of failing." David had a long line of Fs on the report card of life. He tried to deny he'd done anything wrong, until Nathan nailed him with the truth. In Psalm 51 he cried out for mercy, forgiveness, and for God to "restore to me the joy of your salvation" (verse 12). He understood he couldn't have joy until he cleansed his conscience. He faced heartbreaking consequences, but after repenting he had peace, knowing his heart was right with his Father.

I praise God for loving me enough to stop me before I fail so badly that I "flunk out," as David did. It's God's way of showing His love for me, just as my parents showed theirs by not ignoring my "forgotten" homework and other acts of disobedience. I pray that I will never become so numb to sin that I cannot accept responsibility for my mistakes and learn from them.

Thank you, God, that "he who conceals his sins does not prosper, but whoever confesses and renounces them finds mercy" (Proverbs 28:13).

a special prayer

Confession really does cleanse the soul, God. Help me to be thankful for those times when I get caught or feel miserable until I confess or make a change. I pray that any consequences I face will strengthen my character in a way that pleases You. Amen.

questions:

Proverbs 28:14 contrasts a person who fears the Lord with one who doesn't. What happens to the person who hardens his heart?

. . . .

. . . .

Write a prayer asking God to keep your heart soft toward what is right and wrong.

. . . .

. . . .

. . . .

. . . .

Describe how you feel when you know you have done something wrong and need to confess.

. . . .

. . . .

. . . .

How do you feel after you've admitted what you did?

. . . .

. . . .

Why do you think it helps to receive some kind of consequences when you do something wrong?

. . . .

. . . .

In what areas are you thankful to your parents for being strict? Why?

. . . .

. . . .

. . . .

dig deeper

1. How have you seen the truth spoken of in Psalm 94:12-13?

. . . .

. . . .

2. What do you think Paul means by godly sorrow in 2 Corinthians 7: 8-10?

. . . .

. . . .

. . . .

How has your need to confess and keep you conscience clean changed since becoming a Christian or growing in your faith?

. . . .

. . . .

. . . .

. . . .

Please Forgive Me

A llie sat in the high school library, rereading Brooke's note.

"I've been feeling guilty for the way I treated you in middle school. I was so mean."

Mean? What an understatement.

In elementary school Allie and Brooke ate lunch together every day, practically lived at each other's homes, and signed their notes "BFF." Then they started seventh grade. Everything changed when Brooke was elected class vice president and found a new group of friends—Rochelle, Kathleen, and Krista, the cool girls.

About the same time, Allie started gaining weight and breaking out. Wasn't it bad enough that her body seemed to be in a cruel state of rebellion, while Brooke grew more beautiful by the day? The whispers and nasty comments that she overheard from Brooke's new friends made it 10 times worse. Why didn't Brooke stick up for her?

One day during science class Brooke slipped Allie a card. "It's an invitation to Krista's 13th birthday party."

Finally! Brooke must have talked to Krista and the other girls. She pictured Brooke taking the group aside. "Allie is my best friend. As class vice president, I order you to be nice to her!"

Allie got new PJs especially for the party. To her relief, her skin took a turn for the better. Maybe she would run for student government next year too, now that she was in!

It's a game

When Allie arrived at the party, Krista taped a paper to her back. "It's a game. You try to guess what animal you are by asking questions that have 'yes' or 'no' answers. The first girl to guess her animal name wins. Oh, and you go by that name for the rest of the party."

Each girl laughed when she read Allie's back, including Brooke. Twenty minutes later Allie learned her animal name—cow. All the other girls were cute animals—panda bears, kittens, koalas. It was all Allie could do to hold back the tears when even Brooke followed the rule and called her "Cow" until the party ended the next morning.

"It's been three years, and I still can't believe how low I sank with those girls," Brooke's note continued.

"Me neither," Allie whispered. Since then she had lost weight and found new friends. But she'd never forgotten the humiliation of that night at Krista's party, or the pain of seeing her best friend turn on her.

"I asked God to forgive me. Now I'm asking you. Allie, I am so sorry. Please forgive me."

Allie knew that as a Christian she should forgive Brooke. Three years ago she had prayed for this moment. Now that she had the apology in front of her, forgiveness didn't seem so simple.

guilty

mean

nasty

pain

forgive

guilty

mean

nasty

pain

forgive

How could she pretend all that stuff didn't happen? Had Brooke changed or did she only want to clear her conscience?

Allie looked up and spotted Brooke sitting alone at a table on the other side of the library. This would be a perfect chance to talk to her.

"God, I don't know if I can."

Think about the meanest thing that anyone ever did to you. If that person asked for your forgiveness today, how would you react?

When it comes to some situations, forgiveness may seem impossible. Sometimes my only motivation to forgive is obeying Jesus' command to forgive. Even remembering all the times that God has forgiven me doesn't always help. I want to scream, "I never did anything this awful to someone!" It's twice as hard if the person doesn't apologize or ask for forgiveness.

How did Jesus forgive so easily? His disciples deserted Him in His moment of greatest need. His enemies tortured Him, but before they finished killing Him, He cried, "Father, forgive them."

Of course it helped that Jesus was God. None of what happened came as a surprise to Him. He knew the hearts of everyone involved and how God would use each betrayal for His glory. Still, that kind of forgiveness is beyond my comprehension.

All I know is that God tells me to forgive and shows me through example that it's possible

even in the most horrific circumstances. I have also accepted that when I can't forgive, the one who
suffers most is myself.

For me, forgiveness is often a process. Maybe that's what Jesus meant when He said to forgive "seventy times seven" (Matthew 18:22, NASB). He knew it was one thing to say, "I forgive you" and another to let it go. Memories don't erase so easily. When my mind replays details of someone's cruelty, I have to stop and pray, "God, help me to let go of that."

This doesn't mean denying the past. I don't need to suddenly become best friends with the Brookes in my life. The way I see it, forgiveness is refusing to be a prisoner of bitterness, whether my enemy is sorry or not. Each step brings more freedom from the pain, making the next opportunity to forgive a little easier.

A special prayer

God, only You can heal the pain of the cruelty I have endured, but I know that the process must start with me. Help me to forgive those who have hurt me, whether they ask or not. Free me from bitterness, filling that place with the joy I have been missing. Amen.

questions:

Write about a time when you struggled with forgiving someone. . . . .
. . . .
. . . .
. . . .
. . . .

Why was it so hard?
. . . .
. . . .
. . . .
. . . .
. . . .

joy

What happens to you on the inside when you can't forgive?

. . . .

. . . .

. . . .

Why do you think forgiving others is so freeing?

. . . .

. . . .

. . . .

dig deeper

According to Psalm 130:3-4, none of us deserve forgiveness. How might this passage help you when it's time to forgive someone?

. . . .

. . . .

. . . .

Read Matthew 18:21-22. Who do you struggle the most to forgive and why?

. . . .

. . . .

. . . .

. . . .

. . . .

. . . .

Write this passage down on a card or other reminder that you can keep with you.

Friends

always there
for me

Jennifer and I were barely three years old when we met, but the details of that day are still vivid. My family had just moved to a new town. Grandma had taken me outside, probably to get me out of Mom and Dad's hair. Grandma pointed out a little girl standing near the carport of our new apartment building.

"Why don't you go say hello to that little girl," Grandma suggested.

So we walked over. The girl was clutching a doll that looked like a doll I had too.

"Hi, I said. I was about to say, "I have that doll," when she turned and ran home crying.

The next day I saw her again and basically had a repeat of our first meeting. I honestly can't remember when Jennifer warmed up to me. I just know that one day we were mixing dirt and water in a plastic pitcher and calling it juice. We tasted it. This time we both ran home crying. It was supposed to taste like grape!

We have been friends ever since that muddy mix-up. My family moved away when I was eight, but even distance didn't break us apart. Jennifer seems just like family, and I thank God I have a childhood friend who was and is always there for me.

Then there are the friends who came my way exactly when I needed them. God sent Susan when I needed someone to make me laugh. When I moved from California to Reno, Nevada and was lonelier than I had ever been in my life, I met Lynn and Kathy. Then Kari came along. God sent Sherry (not my sister, a different Sherry) to help me through a rough time. In the process we realized that we had a lot in common and now have a special bond.

Carolyn is my "coffee buddy." Kaydie, Peggy and Diane are my writing buddies. Now Gracie is my new "little sis" in Christ.

Each of these friends holds a special place in my heart that no other could fill. Some know me more deeply than others. For example, Kathy has this almost scary way of seeing right through me.

Kathy: How are you doing?

Me: Pretty good.

Kathy: Are you lying? Because you look like you're lying.

Me: (No words because I am now crying.)

Susan always seems to sense when I need to get out and have fun. Once she even kidnapped me.

I know who to call when I need to laugh and who to call when I need to cry or unload.

For a while it seemed like Susan and I did a lot together. Then she got busy and I spent more time with Kari. But, as I've learned through my life-long friendship with Jennifer, time apart doesn't seem to matter for true, faithful friends.

Of course, Jesus is the Friend Who knows me best and loves me most. I know that He is the One I can and should run to first. When nobody else understands what I am feeling or thinking, He not only gets it, but He also cares. Still, I am thankful He has blessed me with friends. They are His living reminders to me that He does not intend for His children to tough out life on their own.

vivid

grape

rough

scary

unload

vivid

grape

rough

scary

unload

I've tried doing that—determined to get through a problem or a bad day, "just me and God." Sometimes that's exactly what I need to do. Other times, He lets me see that, yes, He can meet all my needs, and today one of my needs is a friend. The phone rings and Kathy or Susan is on the line. I go to church for an activity and run into Sherry, who gives me a much-needed hug.

The Bible is full of beautiful examples of Godly friendships: David and Jonathan, Paul and Barnabas, Jesus and His disciples. Hey, if the Son of God saw a need for friends . . .

I love what Ecclesiastes 4:9-12 has to say about friendship:

Two are better than one,
because they have a good return for their work:
If one falls down,
his friend can help him up.
But pity the man who falls
and has no one to help him up! . . .
Though one may be overpowered,
two can defend themselves.
A cord of three strands is not quickly broken.

And what is that third strand? The God who holds the friendships together that He created.

Take some time to thank God, right now, for the special people He has brought in and out of your life, and for those He has waiting for you in the future.

A special prayer

God, thank You for the precious friends that You have sent throughout my life, even those I got to enjoy only for a little while. I praise You for my most faithful friend of all—Your Son, Jesus. Thank You for not forcing me to walk through this crazy, up-and-down life alone. Amen.

questions:

List the names of your closest friends. (It's okay if you have only one. Sometimes it's better to have one good friend.) ....

....

....

....

Devote some time each day this week to pray for them.

Think of one friend who you are particularly close to. Why do you think God placed you in each other's lives?

....

....

....

Who do you go to when . . .
You want to laugh?

....

....

You need to unload?

....

....

You need to cry?

. . . .

. . . .

You have a problem and need advice?

. . . .

. . . .

You want to hang out and do something fun?

. . . .

. . . .

You need someone to pray for you?

. . . .

. . . .

Are some of these people adults? Remember God sends us friends in a variety of age groups. One of my best friends is the same age as my parents.

Maybe you feel like you don't have any friends. Why do you have a hard time making them?

❑ I'm shy.

❑ I move a lot.

❑ I don't fit in at school.

❑ My best friend recently moved.

❑ I'm not sure why, but I really want friends.

❑ Some other reason . . . .

. . . .

. . . .

. . . .

Commit your need for friends to God. Ask Him to send someone your way who is so perfect, you know she came as a gift from Him.

dig deeper

What does the Bible say about friendship in . . .

Proverbs 13:20 . . . .

. . . .

Proverbs 27:6 . . . .

. . . .

Read John 15:9-17. What does this tell you about your relationship with Jesus?

. . . .

. . . .

Write about a time when your friends couldn't be there for you, but Jesus helped you in a special way.

. . . .

. . . .

. . . .

. . . .

. . . .

. . . .

. . . .

. . . .

. . . .

. . . .

. . . .

Key Ingredients

spoon-sized
balls of
cement

"I should tell you this right away."

Jennifer dropped her suitcase beside my bed.

"What?" I flopped into a chair. I had been looking forward to my best friend's weekend visit for a month. Was something about to spoil it?

Jennifer sat on the bed, looking very serious.

Oh no. What if she had a test on Monday and needed to study all day Saturday? That could not happen! I had finished my homework early especially for this weekend.

"I have given up all sweets. Actually, I am not eating junk at all."

Phew! At least we won't spend Saturday at the library. But wait. Give up sweets? I wanted to stand up and yell, "Are you nuts?" I settled for a polite. "Oh, good for you! That must be tough."

Jennifer was the only 16-year-old I knew who would even consider eliminating great things like ice cream, candy, and chips from her menu. If only I could be so disciplined. I figured if she could handle it, I could try for a weekend. Maybe I would really like healthful eating and go on a junk-free diet too. I hoped Jennifer wouldn't notice the gooey cake that I had baked to celebrate her arrival.

I must admit, I really missed our usual trip to the Cold Stone

joy

serious

spoil

sweets

cookies

urge

serious

spoil

sweets

cookies

urge

Creamery. At the movies, Jennifer ordered popcorn without butter, so of course, I did too. I figured this anti-sugar campaign would put an end to our tradition of making cookies whenever one of us stayed at the other's house, but on Sunday afternoon we both got an uncontrollable urge to bake.

"Let's try making some cookies without sugar," Jennifer suggested.

"Yeah!" I guess I was in the mood for a challenge because I seriously felt excited about the idea. I imagined our cookies emerging from the oven, steaming hot and smelling like heaven. Mom and Dad and my sisters would gobble a batch down before we got them off the cookie sheet, and beg for more.

"Mm, these are delicious!"

"I can hardly tell they're healthy."

"How did you make them so sweet and tasty without sugar?"

Good question; how would we make them sweet? I rummaged through the cupboard and came up with three packets of artificial sweetener. Jennifer tossed in a few handfuls of low-fat granola and a scoop of corn meal. Instead of butter we used unsweetened applesauce. For a little extra spice, I added a teaspoonful of cinnamon.

The dough had a pasty consistency and fell onto the cookie sheet like spoon-sized balls of cement. Hopefully they would taste better than they looked . . .and smelled.

Ding went the timer.

Out came the cookies.

We sampled our creation. I practically gagged on the dry, grainy chunk in my mouth. I managed a semi-enthusiastic, "Mm."

Jennifer chewed with the critical palate of a master food critic. "Not bad."

My parents and sisters each tried one, hiding their urge to spit out every last crumb.

That night, after Jennifer left, Sherry and Kristy and I dumped those rocks into the garbage and broke out the cake. I had never appreciated chocolate so much in my life.

It wasn't long before Jennifer was back on sugar too. Several months later I smiled with relief as I watched her savor a big, peanut-butter-filled, chocolate Easter egg. Yum!

Some ingredients just can't be duplicated. No matter what you throw in to replace them, something is always missing. In the end, the results are tasteless, dry, and completely unsatisfying.

I've found that the same is true in my spiritual life. If I want to truly enjoy and get the most out of each day, there are certain ingredients that I simply must have.

If I miss my quiet time, for example, I go the rest of the day with a hunger that I just can't fill, no matter what I try. Other times, I skip reading my Bible and jump right to the devotional book, figuring, it's better than nothing. At least it's spiritual. Even then, something is lacking—a richness that can come only from the inspired Word of God.

If I dive into my day, without taking time to pray and really spend time with God, I miss that sweetness. Sure, I can spend time with my Christian friends, telling them what I would have told God. It's nice, but it isn't the same.

As a child of God, I need to be fed by the sweet, delicious things He says through Scripture. When I take the time to really be with God and refuse to settle for "not bad," life tastes the way it's supposed to. Okay, each day isn't always a gooey piece of chocolate cake, but at least I have peace, knowing that I have gotten what my soul so desperately needs.

A *special prayer*

God, why do I fill up on mediocre substitutes when You provide all the nourishment and treats that I need? I wonder why I feel empty and "not quite right." Help me to crave time with You, the truth of Your Word, and fellowship with Your people. Fill me today. Amen.

questions:

When your life feels dry and unsatisfying, what do you try to fill it with? Be honest. ....
....
....

Chances are, you don't make conscious choices such as, "I think I'll stop praying for a while," or "This quiet-time thing is getting old. Maybe I'll give it up." It happens gradually. What most often keeps you from praying or spending daily time with God? ....
....
....
....
....

What needs to happen in order for you to desire these things in your life again?

. . . .

. . . .

. . . .

. . . .

How does time in God's Word nourish your soul?

. . . .

. . . .

. . . .

. . . .

Mark 1:35 shows us that Jesus started His day with prayer. How is a day that begins with prayer different from one where you skip right to the first thing on your to-do list?

. . . .

. . . .

. . . .

. . . .

dig deeper

Read Psalm 63:1-3.

Think of a time when you seriously thirsted for and longed for God. What was going on in your life?

. . . .

. . . .

. . . .

How did His presence make a difference?

. . . .

. . . .

How did the truths in His Word help you?

....
....
....

How did prayer affect your attitude and help keep you on track?

....
....
....

Write a prayer asking God to create a thirst in you again. ....

....
....
....
....
....
....
....

Joy? What's That?

hy are you downcast, O my soul?" (Psalm 42:5)

A battle raged in King David's heart. Had the God he loved—the God he thought also loved him—abandoned him? It sure felt that way. In case He was still listening, David cried out to his heavenly Father: "Why must I go about mourning, oppressed by the enemy? My bones suffer mortal agony as my foes taunt me, saying to me all day long, 'Where is your God?'" (Psalm 42:9-10).

Did it help that he could remember so clearly the days when he was "leading the procession to the house of God with shouts of joy and thanksgiving" (Psalm 42:4)?

Many generations later, Jeremiah cried out to God in a similar way. He had every reason to be depressed. God had asked him to deliver an important message to His people and nobody in Israel would listen. Now they were paying the price. With everything he loved and hoped for crashing in around him, Jeremiah's own mistakes replayed in his mind: "I well remember them, and my soul is downcast within me" (Lamentations 3:20).

These two passages may seem like downers, but reading them encourages me. They show me that the greatest heroes of the faith

happiness seemed virtually impossible

got discouraged. They had dark days when they questioned God and doubted themselves. But these men also knew where to look for the hope they so desperately needed.

As he poured his heart out to God, David stopped to consider: "Why are you downcast, O my soul? Why so disturbed within me? Put your hope in God, for I will yet praise him, my Savior and my God" (Psalm 42:5).

Jeremiah grabbed on to the one thing that he knew could keep him going: "Yet this I call to mind and therefore I have hope: Because of the LORD's great love we are not consumed, for his compassions never fail. They are new every morning; great is your faithfulness" (Lamentations 3:21-23).

Their problems weren't erased the moment they said, "But God is good." Life still hurt. The wars around them raged on. More problems would come and they knew it. But they also knew Who was on their side. They understood that no pain or problem lasts forever. Someday they would feel good again because they had a faithful God who loved them.

I have felt like David many times—as if tears had literally become my food. I have also felt like Jeremiah—as if all my efforts were for nothing. But even on dark days there is hope, because I know the source of my help. I can tell my hopeless self, "Put your hope in God."

I remember having to do this one summer

raged

cried

suffer

shout

hope

raged

cried

suffer

shout

hope

morning. I was so down that happiness seemed virtually impossible. To make things worse, my devotional reading for the day was on joy!

Joy? What's that? I didn't know whether to laugh or cry as I turned the page of my devotional book.

But for some reason, I kept reading. I searched my Bible for each suggested verse and read every cheesy quote. Inside, I see-sawed between frustration and unrelenting sadness. Why couldn't I just turn on the joy switch and perk up?

Tears welled up, choking me, when I read the instructions at the end of the chapter, telling me to write a journal entry expressing my joy to God. I pulled out my journal.

Should I even bother? Maybe it'll help to be honest with God.

"God," I wrote. "I am supposed to be expressing my joy right now. But I have none. Please forgive me." Then a sentence just flowed from my pen. "Thank You that in You there is always hope. This sadness won't last forever."

I closed my journal feeling surprisingly better. Even in my despair, I knew in my heart that I always had hope. God had pulled me out of the pit before and He would do it again. I just had to wait, holding on to Him the entire time.

Recently I flipped through that book and found the chapter on joy. Had I really underlined and marked that much? And my journal entry! I hope I never lose it, because it is a living reminder that life is never hopeless, even when it feels that way. In the time between that tearful quiet time and the day I stumbled upon my old book and journal, problems, relationships, and wounds to my heart had healed. God had taught me so much about Himself and about myself that I could honestly thank Him for that difficult summer.

Since then I've had plenty more dark days. I'm learning to stop, like David, and encourage my troubled heart: "Put your hope in God."

A special prayer

God, being Your child doesn't mean that life suddenly becomes easy. Sometimes it's exactly the opposite. When my soul is downcast, like David's, help me to put my hope in You, knowing that eventually I will have plenty of reasons to praise You. Amen.

questions:

What is the most likely to make you feel hopeless or "downcast"?
❏ Failure
❏ A fight with a friend
❏ Problems with parents
❏ Breaking up with a boyfriend
❏ Things not going the way I want
❏ Wanting something I can't have
❏ The way my body looks
❏ Past mistakes
❏ All of the above

What does it usually take to make you feel hopeful again?

. . . .
. . . .

Write about something that is getting you down right now.

. . . .
. . . .
. . . .

Now, write a prayer, asking God to bring to mind some reasons why you can feel hopeful for the future.

. . . .

. . . .

. . . .

List some people who are going through difficult times and pray for them.

. . . .

. . . .

. . . .

dig deeper

Read all of Psalm 42 and Lamentations 3:19-26.

Write down a favorite verse from one or both of the passages to keep with you when you need it. Challenge yourself to memorize it.

. . . .

. . . .

. . . .

Look up the word hope in the dictionary. Write the definition here.

. . . .

. . . .

. . . .

Now look up 1 Timothy 4:10 and 1 Peter 1:3.

How do those verses make hope more real to you?

. . . .

. . . .

How is hope different for the Christian than for those who don't have Christ?

. . . .

. . . .

Part of Who I Am

I could
find out a
little about
who she was

My charm bracelet says a lot about who I am. I have my initial—J—and my birthstone—an emerald. The rest of the charms represent things I especially enjoy. One charm has music notes. Another has the comedy/tragedy theatrical masks. Since red is my favorite color, I had to get a red heart. (How did I ever choose a favorite color without seeing any colors? It's a long story.) Other charms include a coffee cup, a rose, and a stack of books that tells the world I am a bookworm.

When these bracelets first became trendy, they were great conversation starters. Someone I hardly knew might notice it, grab my wrist, and say, "Oh, what charms do you have?"

If she also had a bracelet, I could find out a little about who she was through her tiny picture charms.

That's why I made sure to get two charms that reveal my faith—a cross and one that says "I ♥ Jesus."

Friends, acquaintances, and strangers who take a moment to examine my charm bracelet can see that I am someone who trusts and lovess Christ. It's a part of who I am—the most important part.

Last year a friend loaned me a wonderful novel by Randy Alcorn called Safely Home. It's the story of a man in China who is jailed, tortured, and martyred for his faith. Not once does this man or his family let the fear of persecution keep them from staying faithful to Christ and sharing Him with

joy

others. I put myself in their place. Would I be as bold and courageous if my faith could cost me my life? Would I wear a symbol of Christianity, like a cross or an "I ♥ Jesus" charm?

I closed the book feeling like a pretty shallow believer, knowing how likely it was that, put in such a situation, I might keep my faith quiet. But instead of slipping into a pit of self-loathing, I took it as an opportunity for praise: "Thank You, God, that I don't need to live in fear for being a Christian, or for refusing to compromise my faith."

It had been a long time since I really thought about how blessed I am to live in a country where I can wear a bracelet with a cross on it and the phrase "I ♥ Jesus." I can read my Bible in public, go to church when and where I choose, and share with anybody what Christ has done for me. I can blast Christian music at home or in the car, even with the windows rolled down. People might laugh or yell, "Turn that down!" But they won't arrest me or beat me up on the spot for it.

If I give into the pressure to say what is politically correct, it is completely my choice, not something I must do in order to protect my safety. Let this motivate me to be bolder for You, God. Let me wear my faith in more areas than a bracelet that will eventually go out of style.

Obviously I am proud of my faith, but I

charm

music

color

reveal

shallow

charm

music

color

reveal

shallow

also have a tendency to say what I think people want to hear, for fear of offending them. I shrink at the idea of witnessing, knowing that it means answering tough questions like, "Does God really send people to hell?"

If being a Christian is such an important part of my life, then shouldn't that include proudly standing for the truths that go along with my faith? If someone asks me why I believe what I do, shouldn't I be as eager to share as I would be if she asked about music or books?

Praise God that by His grace, I can. I'm finding the more I appreciate how easily He could have placed me in a different country, or even a less Christian-friendly time period, the more excitement I feel when I do have an opportunity to be bold for God's sake. Sure, it's still scary. But the peace that comes makes the temporary fear bearable.

I continue to pray for a greater willingness to stand for Him. When I show the world, "I'm a Christian," I want it to shine through more than jewelry. I hope my commitment to Christ will show more and more through my choices, attitude, and answers to the toughest questions. It's one thing to thank God for giving me such a safe environment in which to be a Christian and another to take full advantage of the privilege.

A special prayer

God, how can I thank You for the gift of faith? Forgive the times I let fear hold me back from sharing Your truth. You have placed me in a safe place to live the Christian life. Let that drive me to speak up for You more often. Amen.

joy

questions:

How do the following things reflect your likes, dislikes, and interests?

Your bedroom . . . .
. . . .
. . . .

Clothing or jewelry . . . .
. . . .
. . . .

The inside of your locker . . . .
. . . .
. . . .

Book covers, folders or other school supplies . . . .
. . . .
. . . .

Your backpack . . . .
. . . .
. . . .

Your car . . . .

. . . .

. . . .

How do you display your commitment to Christ?

❑ Jewelry

❑ A bumper sticker on my car

❑ Pictures in my room

❑ I write Bible verses on my book covers.

❑ I always have my Bible with me.

❑ Some other way . . . .

❑ I don't really display it with a specific thing.

How have these things created opportunities to share your faith?

. . . .

. . . .

. . . .

How have they encouraged you personally?

. . . .

. . . .

. . . .

How has knowing that people see you wearing or displaying symbols about God
kept you on track? . . . .

If there were no such things as Christian jewelry, T-shirts, or bumper stickers, and
quoting scripture in public was illegal, how would you make your faith known to
people around you? . . . .

. . . .

. . . .

Think about the last time that you had a chance to stand up for your faith, witness or boldly share truth. How did you respond to the opportunity?

. . . .
. . . .
. . . .

How did you feel later?

. . . .
. . . .
. . . .

How does the excitement of knowing that you live in a country that allows you to openly follow Christ affect your boldness for Him?

. . . .
. . . .
. . . .

dig deeper

Read Jeremiah 9:23-24.

List some things about you that are easy to talk or brag about.

. . . .
. . . .
. . . .

According to verse 24, what should a Christian be most eager to brag about?

. . . .
. . . .
. . . .

List some practical ways that you can apply verse 24.

. . . .
. . . .

joy

Read Deuteronomy 6:5-9.

In what ways can you make your commitment to Christ more a part of your everyday life?

. . . .

. . . .

. . . .

When you eventually marry and have kids, how do you plan to pass your faith on to your children?

. . . .

. . . .

. . . .

. . . .

. . . .

The Right Thing

he had other
things on his mind

I gripped the phone to keep my hands from trembling. Again I mentally rehearsed the words I knew needed to be said: "Sean, I'm sorry. I can't go to the prom with you."

He will be so mad—mad and hurt.

We had broken up weeks ago. Still, Sean invited me to his senior prom. At first I was excited. It might be fun to go as friends. I pictured us arriving with the group from marching band that Sean usually hung out with. We'd have a great time dancing and going to dinner. I had my eye on a gorgeous dress.

But the more Sean talked, the more I feared that he had other things on his mind for prom night—not just dinner and dancing. He didn't actually come out and say it. I just got an icky feeling whenever he brought up the prom, especially when he said, "Even though we aren't together anymore, we can still . . . you know . . .enjoy ourselves, right?"

At the time I'd said, "Yeah, sure we can." But that statement kept echoing in my mind. His tone had been pretty suggestive when he said, "Enjoy ourselves."

Oh, it's not like we'll be alone, I kept telling myself.

Then again, Sean didn't actually come out and say we were riding to the prom with his friends. I just assumed it. What if he pulls one of those prom-night-horror-story moves and rents a hotel room or drives me to a deserted area?

joy

Oh, he knows me better than that. Besides, the dance sounds like so much fun! I already said I would go.

Then why can't I feel good about this?

I talked to friends and to my sisters. "Wouldn't it be mean to back out? I think he already bought the tickets."

They basically said the same things: "Why waste money on a dress for a night you have a bad feeling about?" "Call him while he still has time to find another date." "You broke up for a reason."

I kept coming back to the two top reasons why Sean and I broke up in the first place. Reason one: He didn't respect my beliefs. Reason two: He was always pushing my limits on affection. Why should I expect prom night to be any different? If anything, he might lay on even more pressure, with the fancy dinner, me in a hot new dress, and countless opportunities to slow dance.

I felt the same way I had on the day I called to break up with Sean—dreading hurting him but deep down knowing I'd be miserable if I didn't say those difficult words.

I finally gathered my courage and dialed Sean's number.

Later that night, I cried over Sean's angry reaction and the knowledge he might miss his senior prom.

enjoy

fun

hot

dance

regret

enjoy

fun

hot

dance

regret

"You did the right thing." Mom tried to comfort me. "He'll find another date."

"I know." And I honestly did know I did right thing. As bad as I felt for Sean, the weight on my heart had lifted, making room for peace.

To this day, the only regret I have is accepting Sean's invitation in the first place. I should never have set him up for disappointment and the stress of trying to find another date at the last minute (though he did find one, to my huge relief). Sometimes I picture what might have happened if I hadn't listened to my heart and the advice of those who cared about me. I might have regretted that date for the rest of my life.

Sometimes inner turmoil is the only way that God can get my attention. I am grateful for those times He wouldn't allow me to be happy until I took the difficult road to His best for me, saying "No" and breaking off a bad relationship. It's never fun. I hate the hurt feelings and confrontations that come along the way (two problems I might avoid if I listen to that still small voice in the first place). But He never fails to send the assurance and comfort I need when I risk doing the right thing.

I pray I'll do the right thing more quickly each time I face the choice, knowing that when I do, I'll be happier in the long run.

a special prayer

joy

God, so often doing the right thing means doing the hard thing. Thank You for the times You have given me the strength for those tough talks. Help me do what I know is right more quickly and stop allowing fear to hold me back. Amen.

questions:

Write about a time that doing the correct thing involved hurting someone's feelings or risking confrontation.

....

....

....

....

How did you feel inside before you took that difficult step compared to afterward?

....

....

....

How has God rewarded you for doing the right thing even when it hurt?

....

....

....

How much power does the fear of confrontation have when it comes to making difficult decisions?

....

....

....

....

joy

Read Luke 6:12-16.

What did Jesus do before making a huge decision?

. . . .

. . . .

Whose feelings did He most likely hurt?

. . . .

. . . .

How does prayer play into your decision making?

. . . .

. . . .

. . . .

. . . .

Read Philippians 1:9-11.

How has your faith changed your view of what is best for you?

. . . .

. . . .

How does the advice of family, friends, and other Christians help you to discern what is right?

. . . .

. . . .

. . . .

If you have a difficult decision to make, ask God for the strength to do what is right. List three friends who you can ask to pray for you.

. . . .

. . . .

. . . .

joy

Perfect

five more pounds
and you'll look
perfect

The numbers on my bathroom scale had never looked better. Ten pounds gone—yes!

Not that I was ever overweight. But I wanted to be thin like the women in fashion magazines and the tiniest girls in my dance class. With my new and improved body, I'd probably get better parts in school plays, attract a great guy, and enjoy life more in general.

The next time I shopped for jeans, I experienced the thrill of buying a smaller size—two sizes smaller, to be exact. Friends actually referred to me as "skinny." Then one day someone made a comment that changed everything: "You look great. I bet if you lose five more pounds you'll look perfect!"

That innocent statement echoed in my mind. Lose five more pounds and you'll look perfect. Perfect!

No longer satisfied with ten pounds lighter, I went for another five. I'm surprised my scale didn't die from overuse. I ate as little as I could get away with. I'll confess that had been my weight-loss method from the beginning (not recommended), but now I lied and picked my way to consuming even less. When the scale hit my desired number, I waited to feel perfect.

It didn't happen. So I lost more.

Suddenly, instead of giving compliments, friends asked, "Are you sick?" My sister said with disgust, "Your arms remind me of refugees in National Geographic."

Wait, what about perfect?

Inside I never stopped feeling dumpy. Would I ever look at my body and like what I saw? It wasn't until I recognized I had a major problem and learned to love myself for more than numbers on the scale that I saw how damaging my quest for the perfect body had become. Now I wonder how I ever lived like that. Besides the constant hunger, I was never satisfied or happy and was constantly scrutinizing my appearance, comparing it to the skinniest—and probably most unhealthy—women in the world.

That perfectionist still lurks inside me. She just zeros in on other things besides weight. Does my hair look perfect? What about my makeup? And my clothes; do they match exactly right? Are they stylish enough?

Performing is another area where I can be extremely hard on myself. If I sing a solo in church, I worry, not because so many people are watching, but because I might not be perfect. What if I'm not as good as the soloist who sang last week? What if, for the first time in all my years of singing, I forget the words? I can beat myself up for days over one quiver in my voice or a weak note. Even if 20 people flag me down to say, "That was beautiful. It really ministered to me," that imperfection haunts me.

Recently the leader of my Sunday school

pounds

tiniest

fashion

sick

hunger

pounds

tiniest

fashion

sick

hunger

class said something that I really needed to hear. He pointed out that God doesn't expect us to be perfect. Only He is perfect. Nobody in the Bible was perfect, except Jesus. God asks His children to be obedient. Sure, I knew that, but I think God wanted to give me a refresher course.

God and I have been doing a lot of work on the perfectionism thing. He keeps reminding me of my Sunday school teacher's words and bringing to mind certain questions.

Do I expect the same perfection from others that I demand of myself? Of course not! My friends can mess up all they want, and I still love them. How many mistakes has God struck me down for? So far, none.

Does striving for perfection make my life easier and serving God more enjoyable? Far from it! I'm a mess. Worse yet, I am completely self-focused. Being my best for God takes a back seat to "Do I measure up? Am I the best, the skinniest, the prettiest? Have I disappointed anyone?" Me, me, me, me.

Since learning to let go of the need for perfection, I have noticed some wonderful differences. When I relax before I sing, for example, and focus on communicating the message in the song instead of my fear of making a mistake, I actually sing better. It's also a lot more fun. Who knew?

When I concentrate on being healthy instead of having the perfect body (however that's defined), I feel a thousand times better. I have energy for what I want to do.

When my expectations aren't so warped, I can meet my goals and end the day satisfied with myself. I can see my strength without all the "weaknesses" blocking my view.

This is an area where I may always struggle. I look forward to that first day in heaven when I will be perfect. But praise God that He doesn't ask it from me now.

a special prayer

God, You accept me in all my imperfection. Why do I so often let my fears, insecurities, and need for acceptance take over? Heal the damage of warped expectations, whether they are someone else's or mine. Help me be satisfied in being my best for You alone. Amen.

questions:

In what areas might some consider you a perfectionist?

❑ Your physical appearance

❑ Academic achievement

❑ Organization

❑ Cleanliness

❑ Your talents and abilities

❑ Your spiritual life

❑ All of the above

Some other area . . . .

. . . .

. . . .

. . . .

. . . .

Do you think your expectations are reasonable? Why or Why not?

. . . .

. . . .

. . . .

Where do you think these high standards come from?

. . . .

. . . .

What is your response when someone else makes a mistake or has standards that are lower than yours? . . . .

. . . .

. . . .

When has your need for perfection taken a toll on . . .

Your health? . . . .

. . . .

Your relationships with others? . . . .

. . . .

Your moods? . . . .

. . . .

Your feelings about yourself? . . . .

. . . .

Your relationship with God? . . . .

. . . .

Maybe you aren't a perfectionist. Why do you think this is? (Note: Believe me, it's not a bad thing.) . . . .

. . . .

. . . .

What do you think the difference is between striving for excellence and unhealthy perfectionism? . . . .

. . . .

. . . .

. . . .

dig deeper

Our Lord Jesus was perfect in every way. Yet what imperfection might some have seen in Him, according to Isaiah 53:2-3?

. . . .

. . . .

. . . .

What does this tell you about God's idea of perfection?

. . . .

. . . .

. . . .

When Paul writes about aiming for perfection in 2 Corinthians 13:11, what area of life is he talking about? . . . .

. . . .

. . . .

. . . .

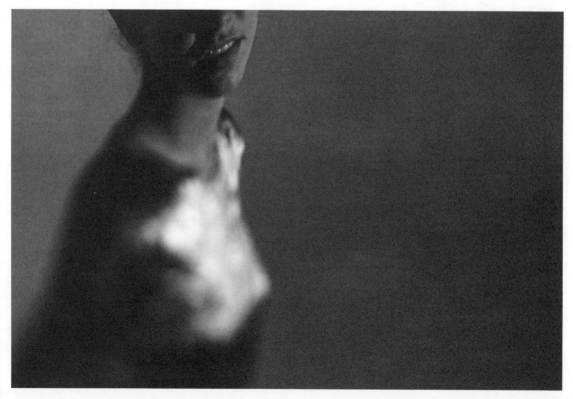

Never Out of His Reach

he felt a hand
grab him out of
mid-air

My sisters and I used to beg Grandma, over and over again, "Tell the story about the time when Great-grandpa Jake almost fell off the roof."

I knew the story down to the tiniest details. It happened on a drizzly day when our family's vacation cabin was being built. Everyone had decided to call it quits for the day, except stubborn Grandpa Jake, who insisted he needed to finish a job he'd started on the roof.

Not long after everyone drove away, he slipped on the slick shingles. Before he knew it he was falling . . . toward an old water heater.

He was sure the end had come. Then he felt a hand grab him out of mid-air and set him gently back down on the roof. Grandpa Jake looked around to see who rescued him. Nobody was there. An indescribable peace covered him. To this day, Grandma insists that an angel pulled her father to safety.

I used to enjoy impressing my friends with this bit of family history: "My great-grandpa was rescued by an angel!"

As I've grown and matured, the story has taken on deeper meaning. It's my reminder of the protective watch that God keeps on His children.

I think of Great-grandpa Jake whenever I read,

> For He will give His angels charge concerning you,
> To guard you in all your ways.
> They will bear you up in their hands,
> That you do not strike your foot against a stone.
>
> (Psalm 91:11,12 NASB)

This passage prompts me to think of the many times when I have experienced a divine hand of protection. I may not have a scenario of my own to brag about that's as dramatic as Great-grandpa's, but it doesn't make me appreciate God's help any less.

I remember a time when Mom and I were driving to the store and stopped at an intersection just as another car whizzed in front of us at top speed.

Mom gasped. "Do you know how easily we could have just been killed? Technically I didn't need to stop. I don't even know why I did. If I hadn't . . ."

Another time I was actually hit by a car while walking across a parking lot. It hurt me and scared me. But looking back, minor injuries and rattled nerves aren't so bad when you consider what might have happened. What if the driver had been going faster? When I fell to the ground in front of her front tire, what if she had

fell

hand

gently

angel

police

fell

hand

gently

angel

police

rolled her car over me? I could have fallen differently and hit my head. I knew without a doubt that someone had been watching out for me that morning.

God has been merciful enough to intervene when I made extremely unwise decisions. Here's one embarrassing example. I was out on a date and let the guy talk me into a ride up to a deserted area with "a great view" (Yeah right. Who cares about a view at midnight?) It wasn't long before a policeman drove up, gave us a lecture, and ordered us to go home. That angry policeman may have been my guardian angel. My date was getting a little too affectionate, and I was too timid back then to know how to tell him to stop.

Those are the instances that stick out in my mind. I'm sure there are thousands I don't even know about. Growing up visually impaired, I've probably had more than my share of near misses as I learned to cross intersections and take public transportation independently. God must have had extra angels assigned to me during those years.

To think that God, who keeps the earth revolving, the tides flowing, and the human race from annihilating ourselves, cares enough to guard my safety. Who am I anyway, that He would even notice where I go from one moment to the next? Aren't there more important people to keep an eye on?

According to Psalm 91:14, He does it simply because I know and love Him—because I am His. He protects His children the way good parents go out of their way to protect theirs. This doesn't mean bad things don't happen. But as long as I'm alive, I can praise my ever-present God for His protection. Each heart-stopping experience that leaves me thinking that could have been it can instead remind me that God still has a purpose for me. Close calls can be exciting moments in a way. For whatever reason, that wasn't it.

They can also serve as wake-up calls that I never know when God will take me home. Until that day comes, I can thank Him for watching out for me, from the first day of my life to the last.

a special prayer

Father God, how many times has one of Your angels pulled me out of danger? I could easily let the near tragedies of life fill me with fear. Instead they can fill me with joy, knowing Who rescued me. Thank You that I am never out of Your reach. Amen.

questions:

1. Reflect on a time when you know God protected you from harm. What did this experience tell you about His love for you?

. . . .

. . . .

. . . .

How did it cause you to look at life differently?

. . . .

. . . .

. . . .

How did it motivate you to live for Him?

. . . .

. . . .

. . . .

2. How did Satan try to use the promise of God's protection to tempt Jesus in Luke 4:9-13? . . . . *joy*

. . . .

. . . .

How did Jesus respond? . . . .

. . . .

. . . .

How do you think people today might put God to the test? . . . .

. . . .

. . . .

. . . .

. . . .

dig deeper Read all of Psalm 91. List the promises of protection you find.

. . . .

. . . .

. . . .

. . . .

. . . .

. . . .

What unique security does God promise us as believers in 1 Peter 1:3-5?

. . . .

. . . .

. . . .

. . . .

Getting Away from It All

When I was about six years old, my dad's side of the family built a cabin in the Sierra foothills. It was nothing fancy, just a place to get away. When we wanted to take a snow trip in the winter or fish during the summer, we had free lodging.

Each year I counted down the days until summer when my family could go to the cabin for an entire week to catch fish, swim in the nearby lake, and picnic in a giant redwood forest.

My sisters and I had a favorite tree that we played in and around for hours. As little kids we brought our dolls there. Later, it was a place to sneak off and talk about boys and other girl stuff. When Jennifer or one of my other friends joined us for a weekend trip, and we wanted a break from pesky little sisters, we huddled under the tree with our magazines and teen novels.

One year Mom and Dad decided to skip the big family Christmas get-together at Grandma and Grandpa's and spend the holiday at the cabin. We tromped through the snow and cut down a fresh pine tree, just like a pioneer family. For the first time in our lives we woke up to a white Christmas. It was one of our most memorable Christmases, even if our relatives were irritated with us for ditching them.

Another time we went at Easter. We woke up before dawn on Easter Sunday, walked to Sunset

mismatched furniture, tacky quilts, amateur paintings

Ridge, and had our own sunrise communion service, right there in the middle of God's breathtaking creation. Later we hunted for Easter eggs, hidden under pine needles and in the notches of fallen trees.

Then there was the year my sister Sherry and I both had fights with our boyfriends in the same week. Dreading a three-day weekend with two sulking girls, playing phone tag with guys who would most likely make us cry again, Mom announced, "Pack your stuff. Dad says we're going to the cabin."

The intoxicating smell of evergreens quickly washed away thoughts of "him." We spent the weekend walking through redwood groves, having barbecues on the back deck with birds chirping overhead, and eating candy purchased during our traditional stop at the Candy Kitchen in the old Columbia ghost town. We went home reborn.

The cabin is full of old, mismatched furniture, tacky quilts, amateur paintings, and handmade knickknacks. Apparently the carpet and linoleum have needed replacing for years. I'm always too busy enjoying the place to notice. Who cares about old carpet when I can step outside, smell glorious fresh air, and enjoy the beauty that God provided for free?

Sometimes I wish I had a driver's license, so I could go to the cabin by myself for an extended quiet time. I would thank God for providing my family with a place to spend vacations even when we didn't have any extra money. It was here I learned to appreciate nature, surrounded by evidence of Psalm 104:24: "How many are your works, O Lord! In wisdom you made them all."

During fun family trips I recognized how quickly the sounds and smells of God's natural world renew my spirit. Creation reminds me how great and unbelievably creative He is. I look up at the trees towering over me and think Wow. God made all this! How could anyone say it simply happened, or evolved from a slimy cell millions and millions of years ago? If He can keep creation in order, He can certainly handle my little everyday problems. Noticing the care He takes in giving each creature a home, food, and instincts to protect itself clearly reminds me how much more He cares about His children.

Not everyone has a cozy spot for family vacations, but God has filled the world with a huge variety of places to get away with Him and enjoy what He created. There are the ocean, ponds, rivers and creeks, meadows, parks, mountains, and trails. If we can't escape to the wild outdoors, then we can sit outside in our backyards or on balconies, listening to birds and feeling the breeze.

When is the last time you took a moment

to thank God for your favorite get-away place, whether it's a vacation cabin, a hiking trail, or a lounge chair in your back yard where you always go when you need to think and pray?

Praise Him for the many times He has refreshed your spirit in that place and filled your heart with precious memories.

a special prayer

Wonderful Creator, thank You for filling the earth with reminders of Your power, beauty, and creativity. Thank You for each glimpse of Your goodness that I see around me. You know the exact place I need to be to renew my soul, and I praise You for that. Amen.

questions:

Where does your family go to get away from the stress of everyday life? If you don't take vacations, where would you like to be able to go? . . . .
. . . .
. . . .
. . . .
. . . .

What is your favorite place to enjoy nature and why? . . . .

joy

. . . .

. . . .

. . . .

Write about a specific time when going to this place lifted your spirit.

. . . .

. . . .

. . . .

. . . .

How does nature make God more real to you? . . . .

. . . .

. . . .

. . . .

dig deeper

Read Psalm 148. What wonders of nature provoke you to praise God?

. . . .

. . . .

. . . .

. . . .

. . . .

How do the words of Psalm 104:24-28 strengthen your faith in God's ability to handle any problems in your life? . . . .

. . . .

. . . .

. . . .

. . . .

. . . .

So Much for Sticks and Stones

healing to
the bones

Heather and I were on our way to the store to buy school supplies when two guys passed us and whistled.

I smiled, blushing. Boys didn't usually whistle at me. For a moment, I felt super-model gorgeous.

Then Heather informed me, "They're not whistling at us."

"Oh, they aren't? I expected her to say the homecoming queen and her first runner-up were walking right behind us.

Instead she said, "We're both too ugly." Her words flowed as matter-of-factly as if she'd said, "We're both wearing purple."

I did a quick mental evaluation of my appearance. Okay, I wasn't super-model gorgeous. My skin wasn't exactly flawless that day. Then there were my tacky dark glasses. But I'd done a pretty good job with my makeup and hair that morning and chosen a cute outfit. At least I'd felt cute until Heather spoke up.

A cloud of self-consciousness followed me to the store and through the aisles. I avoided looking at people, especially guys. When the sales lady rang up my folders, binder paper, and gum, she smiled at me. I forced a quick smile before averting my eyes. She probably felt sorry for me, the poor ugly girl.

Heather was as chatty as ever when we stopped

for a frozen yogurt and headed home. Did ugliness not bother her?

Later I told my sisters about what she said.

"Don't listen to Heather," they ordered me. "She probably thought those guys were whistling at you but not her, so she wanted to make you feel bad," Kristy suggested.

I shrugged. "Maybe." And maybe not.

Sherry pointed out, "Heather feels ugly, so she wants you to feel ugly."

I thought about it. Heather's family had very little money, so she didn't have one stylish outfit. My mom had been a beautician before having kids, so she enjoyed teaching us girls about makeup and hair, fun feminine training that Heather clearly never received. Heather's mom also put her down a lot.

I decided to take my sisters' advice. Why let one person convince me of something that I knew wasn't true?

Proverbs 16:24 says, "Pleasant words are a honeycomb, sweet to the soul and healing to the bones." Unfortunately not everyone chooses to use honey-sweet words. Some are more like sour lemons. You've probably tasted more than you'd like to think about.

Where did that "Sticks and stones may break my bones, but words will never hurt me" expression come from anyway? The truth is that

whistle
blush
ugly
tacky
sweet
whistle
blush
ugly
tacky
sweet

joy

words do hurt. When someone puts down your appearance, your clothes, or your best efforts, doesn't it feel similar to being struck with a stick or a stone?

So how do we keep those blows from beating us down? I've learned to take a few things into consideration when I receive one. First, is what the person said true? Am I ugly, stupid, clumsy, or whatever? No!

What if the comment is true? For example, if someone points out that I pull reading material right up to my face, or that I squint a lot, they are correct, even if it does sting to hear them blurt it out as if I'm doing something weird. But does this person understand why I read the way I do?

Heather taught me to consider what might be going on inside a person hurling sour words. Is she only trying to make me feel as bad as she does? If I sense that she is, I can have a little more patience, maybe even an ounce of compassion.

Keeping in mind what my family and true friends say about me also helps. If those who love me say repeatedly, "You're beautiful," and one acquaintance says, "You're funny looking," who can I assume is right?

More importantly, what does God say about me? Would He agree with this person?

Finally, I have to decide, as I did that day with Heather, will I let one opinion do me in? It's pretty easy to. But is that the way I want to live, letting the meanies in my life make or break the way I feel about myself?

Sometimes I need to take only one of these steps. Other times I take them all, then start over and try again until the truth sinks in and God heals the wound.

As often as possible, I now try to surround myself with friends who build me up, rather than put me down. I spend a lot less time recovering from the blows of sticks and stones—time and energy that I can put into more enjoyable things.

a special prayer

God, You know how deeply I have been hurt by unkind words. Help me learn to weed out the lies and replace them with the truths that You have shown me about myself. Help me also to guard my own words, so they'll heal and uplift others. Amen

questions:

Why do you think words have so much power?

....
....
....
....

Think about the last mean comment that someone made to you.
What was it? ....
....

Who said it? ....
....

Why did it hurt so much? ....
....
....
....

How did the comment line up with what you know about yourself? . . . .

. . . .

. . . .

. . . .

How did it compare to what those who know and love you would say? . . . .

. . . .

. . . .

. . . .

How long did it take to shake the comment off? . . . .

. . . .

If you haven't yet, ask God to heal the wound inflicted by those insensitive words.

What happens to your sense of worth and your level of joy when you are able to let
go of the cruel words of others? . . . .

. . . .

. . . .

How does the memory of hurtful words affect the way you speak to other people?

. . . .

. . . .

dig deeper

According to 1 Peter 3:9-10, how should a Christian respond to insults and
put-downs? . . . .

. . . .

What are the rewards? . . . .

. . . .

. . . .

Read Proverbs 25:11. Reflect on a compliment or kind comment that came exactly when you needed it.

What was the compliment? . . . .
. . . .
. . . .

Why was it so helpful? . . . .
. . . .
. . . .
. . . .

Who can you encourage or uplift with your words today? . . . .
. . . .
. . . .

joy

Promises, Promises

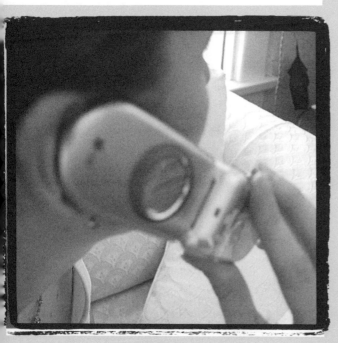

if you buy one of their phones, you're "in."

A beauty article promises that if you follow specific hair and makeup tips, you could look exactly like Kirsten Dunst. Wow! Wouldn't that be nice?

Hey, wait. What about those of us who have completely different hair and coloring from Kirsten? We could end up looking more like clowns than like a beautiful actress. Forget that one, I guess.

A TV commercial promises clear skin in three days. That's not long to wait. As proof, it shows a girl with acne. In the next scene it's a little better. On day three, voila, her face is peaches-and-cream flawless. Amazing!

Okay, let's have a show of hands. How many of you have had a full-blown breakout disappear completely in three days? Uh huh, yeah. Me neither.

How about this one then? According to a cell phone ad, if you buy one of their phones, you're "in." I don't know about you, but I've always wanted to be "in." Everyone in the ad looks happy and popular. And they're all going to a party—a party for "in" people.

Then again, how can a cell phone miraculously make a person more popular? How many times have you seen someone holding a cell phone and thought, Wow, she must be so happy and have lots of friends because she has a (fill in the brand) phone.

Needless to say, the promises of advertising usually can't be trusted. How many times have ads for makeup, skin care, hair thickeners, or the latest technology disappointed you?

People also make a lot of promises they can't keep:

"We'll always be best friends."

"I'll love you forever."

"I'll never hurt you."

Friendships end, whether or not we want them to; love fades; and yes, as much as we try to be kind, we hurt each other. We make promises that we could keep, if we really tried:

"I promise not to tell."

"Sure, no problem. I'll help you with that project."

"I'll make sure you get invited."

Then, for whatever reason, we don't follow through. After all, we are human. We make mistakes, buckle under pressure, and make more commitments than we can keep. Even parents can't keep all of their promises, as much as they would like to.

So whom can we trust to keep their word? Thankfully, there is one Person. We can count on God to come through, every time. And He promises some pretty unbelievable things:

He'll love you forever, be your best friend,

hair

makeup

Kirsten

"in"

hurt

hair

makeup

Kirsten

"in"

hurt

and never hurt you or leave you.

He'll forgive your sins, no matter how badly you mess up, and keep right on forgiving even when you make the same mistake over and over.

He promised eternal life in heaven to anyone who trusts in His Son—anyone!

He gives strength to heal from things like addiction, emotional pain, and shame of the past.

He promises to provide for you, and to fill you with peace, comfort, joy, and wisdom whenever you need them.

He promises to do great things in your life, and to actually use you to accomplish His plans.

All this and you don't have to buy anything or knock yourself out trying to earn His blessings. Better still, He means it. Unlike clever advertisers or well-meaning friends, God doesn't lie or say what you want to hear: "For no matter how many promises God has made, they are "Yes" in Christ" (2 Corinthians 1:20).

Are you reeling from a broken promise, or a series of them? Chances are, the next time someone says, "I promise," you'll probably say to yourself, "Right. I've heard that before."

Recently, my family was going through a difficult time. I didn't know what God was doing. I felt disappointed and let down, even by God. A friend gave me some advice: "Cling to His promises."

So any time I felt discouraged or fearful, I

tried. At first it didn't help much. The Bible's promises felt like annoying pat answers. Prove it, God. So I took it a step further and considered how God had kept those promises in the past. How had He provided for me recently? How had He shown His love? What good things had He done through the trial? Before I knew it, I was overflowing with gratitude and hope for what lay ahead. I served a God who would not let me down. Things didn't change right away, but I changed on the inside.

So why not give it a try? Set aside your current disappointment for a moment. Or better yet, cry out to God with your disappointment and pain. Go ahead and be honest. When you're finished, ask God to fill your heart with His promises and to help you cling to them as you watch Him work.

A special prayer

God, I've been let down so many times it's hard for me to believe anyone, even when that person says, "I promise." I thank You that Your promises can be trusted. Help me to trust in them—to cling to them, even when life seems hopeless. Amen.

questions:

In what ways has God shown His love to you this week? Remember that God often shows His love through the kindness of your family or other Christians.

. . . .
. . . .
. . . .
. . . .

How has He provided for you today? (Hint: He doesn't always provide in the way that we expect or ask for.) . . . .
. . . .
. . . .
. . . .
. . . .

What are some of your favorite promises from the Bible and why?

. . . .

. . . .

. . . .

. . . .

. . . .

. . . .

Think of a time when it felt like God wasn't keeping His promise. How did He show you His faithfulness? . . . .

. . . .

. . . .

What did that experience teach you about Him? . . . .

. . . .

. . . .

. . . .

. . . .

. . . .

Sometimes bad experiences with people make it difficult to trust God for what He says He will do. When has this been true for you?

. . . .

. . . .

. . . .

If you still struggle with trusting God, write a prayer asking Him to help you in this area. . . . .

. . . .

. . . .

When have God's promises gotten you through a difficult time?

. . . .

. . . .

. . . .

dig deeper

What does God promise in:

Psalm 145:18-19 . . . .

. . . .

. . . .

Proverbs 3:26 . . . .

. . . .

. . . .

Hebrews 4:16 . . . .

. . . .

. . . .

How has God kept these promises in your life recently?

. . . .

. . . .

. . . .

. . . .

. . . .

List some things that Colossians 2:13-14 assures you of. Thank God for the promises in this verse. . . . .

. . . .

. . . .

. . . .

Add this to your wish list: . . . .
. . . .
. . . .

If you struggle to remember or trust God's promises, buy or ask for a Promise
Bible. Keep it with you to read when you need a reminder that Somebody cares
enough to do what He says He will do.

journal

What I Learned at Summer School

How would I survive the next six weeks?

How had I let myself get talked into this? While our friends spent their summer sleeping in, going to movies, and hanging out at the mall, my sister Sherry and I had been asked to work at a Living Skills program for visually impaired kids.

At first I thought the opportunity sounded fun, especially the part about getting paid. Then the director called. "School begins at 8:00, but it's 20 miles from your house and the driver has several stops to make. So the bus will arrive around 6:30 a.m."

Six thirty? That means getting up at . . . I didn't even want to think about it.

"Look for one of those small buses for disabled students."

Wait! We'd never ridden one of those buses before. Riding the city bus while our friends earned their driver's licenses was bad enough. What if someone saw us piling into it?

That first morning, Sherry and I practically sprinted to the bus. We did not choose window seats.

A few minutes later, the bus made a stop. I immediately recognized the new passenger—Greg. We went to school together. He hardly talked, never

joy

wore deodorant, and teachers were always trying to hook us up because we had the low-vision thing in common. Naturally, he chose to sit next to me. I forced a smile.

Finally, our bus pulled into a crowded high school parking lot. Sherry, Greg, and I escaped the bus. The eyes of every student sentenced to a summer of repeating algebra 1 or English 9 seemed to zero in on us.

How would I survive the next six weeks? Was it too late to back out? But once we found our classroom, memories of that horrible bus ride and getting up with the roosters began to fade.

A dark-haired girl walked over to us, two cute guys following her. "Hi, I'm Stephanie," she said. "This is Eric and this is Wayne." Like my sister and me, all three of them had grown up with poor vision and were assigned to help with the younger kids.

Boys and girls started showing up, wearing the familiar thick or dark glasses. An adult teacher led the one completely blind little boy, his pudgy hand resting on her elbow. All day long the kids swarmed around Sherry and me and the rest of the helpers like we were the coolest people in the world.

Over the next six weeks I recognized how much I would have missed if I had allowed little inconveniences and embarrassment to keep me from a rewarding experience.

paid

6:30

small

pudgy

skills

paid

6:30

small

pudgy

skills

I would have missed out on special friendships with Stephanie, Eric, and Wayne. I would never have experienced the satisfaction of teaching Annie how to cook, giggling with Megan as she learned to paint her nails and arrange her long hair into fashionable styles, and helping Wayne give Peter a crash course in first aid. Many of the kids had been pampered since birth, or told repeatedly, "You can't do it." Each day offered chances to show them how capable they really were.

During that summer program, I discovered how much I loved working with disabled children. After years of receiving skills and help from gifted teachers, I now had something to offer.

And okay, I even learned to appreciate Greg a little more. Kids who some of us couldn't manage responded to his quiet, patient personality. I never would have guessed.

The summer before my senior year of high school could have easily been just another three months of the same old thing. Instead, it included six weeks of friendship, growth, and unexpected fun.

Sometimes it's worth a little inconvenience to grab an opportunity that God is holding out—a chance to serve Him in a new way, discover a hidden talent, touch a life, or have my life touched. How many precious moments have I lost because I didn't want to be bothered, didn't think the plans sounded fun enough, or I didn't want to deal with a person I considered annoying?

Instead of looking back with regret, I look ahead with anticipation for what God has for me next. Will I recognize the next early morning, the next afternoon working alongside my least favorite person, or a change to my summer plans as the divine opportunity that it is?

Wonderful rewards wait when I am willing to set my selfishness aside and stay open to God's agenda. "I am the Lord your God, who teaches you what is best for you, who directs you in the way you should go" (Isaiah 48:17). And I pray that I will always follow His lead.

a special prayer

Father, Your leading doesn't always look like fun at first, but in the end, nothing can compare. Thank You for the exciting adventures that You have taken me on and for those that await me in the future. May I never answer, "No" when You ask me to serve. Amen.

questions:

How quick are you to turn down an opportunity that includes inconvenience or working with someone you don't like? . . . .
. . . .

Think of a time when you wanted to say "No" or back out of a commitment, but followed through anyway. What did you gain from the experience?
. . . .
. . . .
. . . .

When have you been able to pass on to others what someone else taught you?
. . . .
. . . .
. . . .
. . . .

How were you blessed? . . . .
. . . .
. . . .
. . . .

Think of a job or commitment that is coming up. How much are you looking forward to it? Why might God be leading you in this direction?

. . . .
. . . .
. . . .
. . . .

dig deeper

Read Genesis 6:9-22, Mark 14:32-36, and Luke 1:26-38.
How could the future have turned out differently if each of these people had allowed inconvenience, personal discomfort, or fear to keep him or her from saying, "Yes" to God? . . . .
. . . .
. . . .
. . . .
. . . .
. . . .

What did each gain by obeying?

. . . .
. . . .
. . . .
. . . .
. . . .
. . . .
. . . .
. . . .

What did others gain?

....

....

....

....

....

journal

....

....

....

....

....

....

....

....

....

....

....

....

....

....

....

....

....

....

....

A Night of Praise

I should just come right out and spill it all

I t is good to give thanks to the LORD and to sing praises to Your name, O Most High; To declare Your lovingkindness in the morning and Your faithfulness by night.

(Psalm 92:1-2, NASB)

I didn't show up at our church's Sunday evening prayer service to praise God for all the great things that were happening in my life. Instead, to be perfectly honest, I had a pretty long list of prayer requests rolling around in my head. It had been one of those weeks—one of those months, actually—when everything seemed to go the exact opposite of how I planned or wanted.

Okay, how could I condense my list into one general request, so I wouldn't dominate the time? I rehearsed in my mind, trying to come up with a version that sounded the least whiney.

Oh, maybe I should just come right out and spill it all. People do it all the time. Venting might help me feel better. I sat down next to my friend Cole. Her dad had recently passed away, so I gave her a hug.

"How are you doing?"

She smiled. "I'm okay."

Pastor Greg interrupted our conversation. "Instead of our usual prayer time, God has laid it on my heart to have a night of praise. When we praise God, we not only bless Him, but we bless others as well. Never mind the great things that it does for us."

My head drooped. Praise God? What for? Life basically stunk. This unexpected shift in

joy

routine seemed a little unfair. What if someone had a dying relative or a big test tomorrow or just had a lot on her mind, like I did? Were we supposed to suffer in silence?

I tried to mask my disappointment. Oh well. It would be pretty rude to get up and leave. Maybe after the service I could share my prayer needs with someone.

Pastor Greg went first, sharing an exciting thing that happened to his daughter, during their vacation. I looked up. Oh, so the praises didn't need to be for major things. I could probably think of something small. It might look weird if everyone had a praise except me.

Cole raised her hand to go next. If she could find room to praise God, right after losing her dad, then I could certainly come up with a reason. God, help me.

Cole opened her Bible. "God really comforted me through a verse that I read the day that I found out my dad died." She read the passage that God had led her to on that sad day.

Immediately I thought of something that I had read a few days before when I was feeling especially discouraged. A quote that I just sort of stumbled upon had said exactly what I needed to hear. How could I have forgotten? I raised my hand and shared the quote. A smile spread across my face, remembering how much those words had encouraged me.

praise

bless

unfair

suffer

sad

praise

bless

unfair

suffer

sad

More people talked about good things that God had done—answered prayers, family members who had finally accepted Christ, recoveries from sickness. We went around the room again and again, until we ran out of time. I think I shared three praises that night. Nobody wanted the hour to end, including me.

I got up to leave. Oh yeah, I'm going to share my prayer request with someone.

I glanced around. But the need to talk about my problems didn't seem so urgent anymore. In fact, I felt better than I had in weeks. Why ruin it by dwelling on the negative again?

Who knows, maybe God laid the idea for a praise night on Pastor Greg's heart just for me. I didn't need to pour out all that was going wrong. I'd done enough of that in my journal at home. Searching my memory for the small but significant ways that God encouraged, strengthened, and blessed me each day had brought the healing that my spirit needed. Listening to my friends share their own miracles and answers to prayer filled me with reminders of God's goodness and ability to supply all my needs in His way and in His timing.

It is good to give thanks to the LORD.

Even when I think my life is nothing but one big disaster; it is good to give thanks—to rack my brain for something, anything. It may not change my situation, but as Pastor Greg said, it does wonders for my heart. Remembering what God has done in the past gives me hope for what He'll do in the future. Spending time expressing my gratitude shifts my focus from myself to my all-sufficient God.

Why don't I spend time praising and thanking God more often? Why doesn't each prayer time, even when I'm alone, include an extended time of praise?

a special prayer

Heavenly Father, I have so much to be grateful for. If nothing else, I am alive and loved by You, the King of Heaven. Help my "Thank You" list to grow, God. Shift my focus from what I wish could be, to the gifts You have showered me with already. Amen.

questions

How would you describe your life right now?
❑ Great
❑ Good, compared to some of my friends
❑ Okay
❑ Couldn't get much worse
Explain why. . . . .
. . . .
. . . .
. . . .
. . . .

What do you have to thank God for today? . .
. . . .
. . . .
. . . .
. . . .
. . . .

joy

List three prayers that God has answered recently. . . . .

. . . .

. . . .

. . . .

. . . .

. . . .

Now, go back to the second question and see if your answer changes.

. . . .

. . . .

. . . .

Face it. We usually remember the bad stuff for much longer than we remember the good. How can you help your mind hold onto God's goodness longer?

. . . .

. . . .

. . . .

. . . .

CHALLENGE: For the next seven days, record as many praises, answered prayers, and unexpected blessings as you can. Track your mood as you trace God's faithfulness to you.

dig deeper

Read David's song of praise in 2 Samuel 22:1-51.

How has God protected you recently (verses 1-20)? . . . .

. . . .

. . . .

. . . .

. . . .

. . . .

. . . .

joy

When did He help you to obey Him even though it was difficult (verses 21-28)?

. . . .
. . . .
. . . .

How did He reward your obedience? . . . .

. . . .
. . . .

When has God brought you light during a dark time (verse 29)? . . . .

. . . .
. . . .
. . . .

How has He strengthened you recently, or allowed you to do more than you thought possible (verses 30-46)? . . . .

. . . .
. . . .
. . . .

How can you express your thanks to God (verses 47-51)? . . . .

. . . .
. . . .
. . . .
. . . .

joy

What Could Have Been

my family really
was unique

I used to think my testimony sounded pretty boring. I grew up with Christian parents who took me to church from day one. I remember sitting on my bed with Mom at age five and asking Jesus to forgive all my sins (taking my little sister's crayons, sneaking a pack of flowered underwear into Mom's shopping basket because I didn't like the plain ones she had chosen—horrible things like that). I asked Him to come into my heart, and "Please write my name in Your book."

Mom's family tree has pastors and missionaries on almost every branch, so pretty much everyone on her side follows Christ. Dad's parents became Christians as young adults. After that, they made their family their mission field until each loved one accepted Christ. So I didn't even have unsaved relatives to pray for.

As a child, I assumed that everyone believed in God, prayed before meals, went to church on Sundays, and knew they would go to heaven when they died. I'll never forget my shock when Mom told me, "Many people aren't Christians. There are probably more non-Christians in the world. That's why you need to talk to your friends about Jesus, so they can go to heaven too."

The older I got, the more I recognized that my family really was unique. By the time I hit junior high, only two of my friends attended church—Jennifer, who I rarely saw, and Jacqueline, who attended my church.

When I was in high school our family did the unthinkable—we slowly dropped from church attendance. Before we knew it, my sisters and I spent more and more time around nonbelievers. Suddenly, very few of our friends attended church. Instead, they sneaked out at night to go dancing at clubs, watched R-rated movies, drank, and planned parties for when their parents left town. Of course we had to try some of those things too.

I didn't date a Christian guy until I met one through the Bible study group that I started attending in college. One of my boyfriends was actually an atheist and proud of it.

Thankfully, God drew me back before I had a chance to do anything too regrettable. But when kids in the college group shared how God delivered them from drug addiction, wild partying, or a lifetime of being told that He didn't exist, I dreaded the moment when I'd be asked to share my uneventful testimony. It seemed like I'd always been a Christian.

One day I actually had to sit down and write my testimony out. As I looked back, God started to open my eyes to all He saved me from by blessing me with parents who would introduce me to Him at such a tender age and raise me to respect and fear Him. What if I'd been born into one of my non-Christian friend's families instead?

I thought about the phobias that I'd battled since childhood, the eating disorder that I still struggled with on occasion, my insecurities, and tendency to get depressed. If I didn't have God to turn to, how intense would these problems have become? Would I still be

boring

plain

sins

tender

blessing

boring

plain

sins

tender

blessing

here? If so, would I be some kind of scary mental wreck?

Then there were all the guys I'd dated. When I thought about it, I was pretty eager to please them, fearing that they would stop liking me. My foundation of faith kept me from giving in to pressure to go too far for their love.

When my family wasn't attending church, I still had a healthy fear of not obeying Him. I may have done some things that I'm not proud of, but God never let me get too far out of His reach.

The longer I thought and wrote, the more I found myself praising God for His work in my life. Like my friends in the college group, I stood as a trophy of His grace. God knew exactly which parents should raise me, at what age I needed to accept Him as Savior, and what I had to experience in order to get the place where He wanted me.

Though I couldn't remember a time when I didn't know God, I could look back on many lessons that taught me about mercy, grace, forgiveness, and the importance of obedience. I had to learn through trials and tears like every other Christian. Now God and His love are more real than when I was five and inviting Jesus into my heart.

How can a testimony of God's handiwork possibly be boring? Now, if I have the opportunity, I can't wait to share mine!

a special prayer

God, when I think of all You've done in my life, how can I not get excited? Help me to never compare the life You planned for me with another and see mine as less important. The fact that You chose me is enough reason to praise You. Amen.

questions:

Write the story of how you came to Christ. . . . .
. . . .
. . . .
. . . .
. . . .
. . . .

Pray for an opportunity to share your story with someone.

What has God saved you from by leading you to Him? . . . .
. . . .
. . . .
. . . .
. . . .
. . . .

How might your personality, attitude, or choices be different without Christ?
. . . .
. . . .
. . . .
. . . .
. . . .
. . . .

joy

How has your family contributed to your faith? If you are the only Christian in your home, consider how God has used other people.

. . . .

. . . .

. . . .

. . . .

List some people (friends, family, famous people, men and women who have spoken at your church or youth group) who you admire because of their awesome testimonies. . . . .

. . . .

. . . .

. . . .

. . . .

How might God use yours someday? . . . .

. . . .

. . . .

. . . .

. . . .

. . . .

. . . .

Spend some time praising God for the truth that you find in:

dig deeper

Daniel 12:1

Romans 10:8-11

Romans 10:13

Colossians 1:13-14

Hebrews 7:25

Hebrews 10:11-14

Do you ever doubt your salvation or fear that you might lose it? How do some of these passages reassure you? . . . .

joy

. . . .

journal

You Want Me to Do What?

stepping out of
his comfort zone
had been scary

Had Moses heard God correctly? Was the God of the universe really asking him to confront Pharaoh and lead His people out of slavery in Egypt? Why him?

"O Lord," Moses stammered, "I have never been eloquent." He reminded God about his speech limitation. Surely God would get someone else now, someone who knew how to rally the people.

But God refused to let Moses off the hook. "Who gave man his mouth? Who makes him deaf or mute? Who gives him sight or makes him blind? Is it not I, the Lord? Now go; I will help you speak and will teach you what to say" (Exodus 4:11-12).

Still Moses begged God to reconsider.

Instead of having compassion on Moses, God got mad. Did Moses realize whom he was saying "No" to? God assured him that He would provide Aaron as an assistant. Moses' own staff would soon be used to perform miracles. Moses was the one God had chosen. All he had to do was obey.

I wonder what went through Moses' mind all those months later, when he stood with countless Israelites on the other side of the Red Sea, all rejoicing in their newfound freedom. I imagine he was grateful he had obeyed God's calling. Yes, stepping out of his comfort zone had been scary. At times he must have thought, We'll never get out of Egypt. Some days he most likely felt, once again, as if God had chosen the wrong guy for the job. Yet there they stood, free at last.

In time, Moses discovered strength and abilities he never knew he had. He wasn't the same man who had cowered at the thought of God's assignment. He could confront a heartless Pharaoh and lead God's people! And this was just the beginning.

When faced with opportunities I feel unqualified to handle, I respond a lot like Moses. Even if the opportunity is an exciting one, I often panic under the weight of my insecurities. I'm not intelligent enough, eloquent enough, and talented enough.

The first time I really felt dragged out of my comfort zone was in middle school. In eighth-grade English we had to write and perform a speech on a controversial topic. I chose television violence.

"I'll pick three of you to enter the school speech competition," Mr. Kelley informed the class. To my shock, he chose my speech as one of the three. Mine!

Why would he pick me? I was no speaker! It had been scary enough to get up in front of the class to give my speech. But apparently Mr. Kelley thought I had potential to go further. He worked with me and encouraged me, challenging me to speak with authority. He never let me forget he had chosen me for a reason.

The next thing I knew, I was giving my television violence speech in front of the seventh-period English classes—round one of the competition. I didn't make it to round two, but I walked away knowing I'd done a good job.

lead

speech

rally

hook

shock

lead

speech

rally

hook

shock

To this day, I thank Mr. Kelley for asking me to do something I never would have chosen for myself. The experience gave me a shot of much-needed confidence. He helped me discover that I'd been wrong all along; I actually did have a knack for public speaking. I liked being up in front of an audience! I carried my new skill into high school, where I got As in the required speech class that everyone else dreaded taking, won speaking awards, and joined the speech team.

I've been forced out of my comfort zone countless times since then. Each experience was scary. I had my moments of doubt. Sometimes I questioned the sanity of the person who gave me the opportunity: What ever made her think I could do this? But in the end, as with that frightening speech, I was glad I didn't say no.

Each step out of my box allows me to learn something new about myself. I stretch my abilities and my confidence. Most of all, I gain greater appreciation for what I can do through Christ.

When I consider the great heroes of the faith, I realize they didn't do amazing things for God by hiding in their safe, little cocoons. They had to step outside into the dangerous world.

If I want to do great things for Him—and I do—then I must be willing to follow their example, to kiss my shell goodbye, and see what He has waiting for me when I say yes.

a special prayer

God, it would be so easy to limit my life to the safe and comfortable. But so often You ask Your children to step outside the safety zone and try scary things. Lord, give me the strength to say yes when called to do Your work. Amen.

questions:

When have you had to step out of your comfort zone lately? . . . .

What did you gain from the experience? . . . .

How does your relationship with God grow when you rely on His strength to get through something scary? . . . .

List some skills that you never would have discovered if you hadn't been forced out of your comfort zone. . . . .

Where does your true competence come from, according to 2 Corinthians 3:4-5? . . . .

. . . .

. . . .

Why do you think that it helps sometimes to doubt your abilities? . . . .

. . . .

. . . .

. . . .

Read Exodus 3:1—4:17.

What were Moses' fears regarding God's calling? . . . .

. . . .

. . . .

How did God respond to these fears? . . . .

. . . .

. . . .

. . . .

. . . .

. . . .

How would you have responded if you were in Moses' position? . . . .

. . . .

. . . .

. . . .

. . . .

. . . .

. . . .

HANDICAPPED

PARKING ONLY

Leanne

the problem
was mine

All the kids at Pine Valley Middle School tried to be nice to Leanne. Maybe I tried a little too hard. But when you're thirteen and don't have many friends, you do things like that.

Leanne was in a wheelchair. We both took art second period, and had to enroll in a PE class for students with disabilities. Every time I saw Leanne, I made a point of saying, "Hi."

She usually looked at me like I had two heads and responded with a snotty or sarcastic, "Hi."

At first I thought the problem was mine. When I overheard a teacher say that she liked Leanne, I told myself that she must be a likable person. Obviously, I just needed to try harder.

One morning, I saw her at a table in one of our school's open areas.

"Hi, Leanne." I smiled.

She gave me the "why do you have two heads?" look. "Hi."

Okay, at least she is still looking at you. Say more.

"How are you?"

"Uh, fine." It came out like, "Duh, I'm not sick or injured. I'm here, aren't I?"

I did not give up. "So, are you waiting for a class?"

Leanne held on to her firm stare. "Maybe."

Why is this not going well?

What had I done wrong? Okay, maybe "Are you waiting for a class?" was a dumb question. But hey, I was getting desperate! I walked away feeling like I'd been slapped.

That's the last time I saw Leanne. Without giving a reason, she changed schools. I felt guilty about how relieved I was to see her go. No more trying to be nice. No more wondering, What am I doing wrong?

It didn't take long to figure out I hadn't done anything. For whatever reason, Leanne was a miserable girl. While I resented her coldness, I couldn't help feeling sorry for her. How sad that she chose to go through life with such an angry, defensive attitude, even as her peers tried to reach out to her. I knew many kids who struggled with physical limitations, as Leanne did. Others had family problems, deep disappointments, and even abuse at home. Still, they didn't act like Leanne.

Remembering her prompts me to think, How often do I act like Leanne—as bitter as my circumstances? How many times have I sulked about my life, even to the point of pushing away someone who wanted to help lift me out of my pity pit?

I am pretty sure Leanne did not have Christ in her life. If she did, I couldn't tell. Is that a mistake I want people to make with me? Oh yeah, she's a Christian. I keep forgetting. She always looks so depressed.

One thing I've learned—my circumstances are out of my control. I had no say in the way God wove me together, how people would treat me, or how many difficulties I would face in life. My attitude, on the other hand, is completely up to me. I can let the unfairness of life turn me into

snotty

problem

smiled

dumb

deep

snotty

problem

smiled

dumb

deep

a grouch, or I can ask God to help me rise above it and use all that I have experienced for His good.

When I focus on all that is going wrong, especially when I feel surrounded by those who are better off, my mood plummets. When I focus on all that God has done for me, the way He molded and directed me from the beginning, the growth that has come through every trial, the creative ways He shows His love, I can't help reflecting at least a glimmer of His light.

When I have a need and see God meet it through an unexpected source, how can I not let my gratitude show? When I am lonely or down and someone smiles, stops to talk to me, or gives me a hug, not even knowing that I needed one, how can I continue to mope?

The key is choosing to focus on the good instead of on those things I wish were different. When a bad mood hits, or a problem begins to consume me, I have to stop and remind myself, If nothing else, let the hope of Christ come through. You can hurt. You can be mad about what is happening in your life, but don't take it out on the world.

Once in awhile, I think about Leanne. I hope that the kindness of her junior high classmates touched her, even if she couldn't let it show. I pray that she will someday be transformed by the renewing power of the God I love. More importantly, I pray that I will reflect Him daily, no matter how unfair life seems.

joy

A special prayer

God, in You there is always a reason for hope. But when everything seems to go wrong, that truth can be really hard to remember. Fill my mind and heart with reminders of Your grace each day. Help me reflect Your joy, even through the darkest storm. Amen.

questions:

List some people who are living with difficult circumstances (disabilities, health problems, tragic events), but don't seem to be bitter. Why do you think this is? . . . .
. . . .
. . . .
. . . .
. . . .

What can you learn from these people?

Psalm 119:71-74 lists some good things that can come from affliction. How has affliction strengthened your relationship with God? . . . .
. . . .
. . . .
. . . .
. . . .

How does recognizing this help you when facing difficulties? . . . .
. . . .
. . . .
. . . .
. . . .

joy

dig deeper

Read Ruth 1:3-22.

Naomi had endured an unimaginable amount of loss. No wonder she wanted to change her name to one that meant "bitter." Yet Ruth stuck by her side.

Imagine what it must have been like for Ruth to be around that constant grief and negativity. (Keep in mind that Ruth had also lost her husband.) How would you have responded in her situation? . . . .
. . . .
. . . .
. . . .

What do you think kept her from becoming like Naomi? . . . .
. . . .
. . . .
. . . .

Read Psalm 100. Read it out loud, if that doesn't feel too weird.

How do the truths in this psalm change your perspective on anything that is going wrong in your life right now? . . . .
. . . .
. . . .
. . . .
. . . .

What Green Looks Like

I couldn't wait to celebrate

"No eye has seen, no ear has heard, no mind has conceived what God has prepared for those who love him." (1 Corinthians 2:9)

Our speech and debate team had blown away the competition at the district tournament. For the first time all year, I advanced to the finals in dramatic interpretation. Deana and I couldn't wait to celebrate with our roommates at the hotel.

"Let's get some sparkling cider at the store across the street." Deana tugged on my arm.

After finding the cider and some snacks, Deana pointed me toward the party supply aisle. "We'll need some cups—cute ones."

Deana and I browsed the shelves, and I spotted what looked like a pretty plastic glass.

"Ooh, how about this?" I held up my great find. "They're marked down to 10 cents each."

Deana wrinkled her nose. "That's because they're ugly."

I looked the glass over. What was wrong with it? "They are?"

Deana took the glass out of my hand and set it back on the shelf. "They're very . . . green."

"Isn't green a pretty color?"

"Not that shade."

Deana chose a pack of cups that had a flowery design on them. A feeling that I had grown pretty accustomed to over the years came over me: the "it's a color thing; you'll never understand" feeling. Since childhood I had tried to figure out the world of colors and shades, but it all seemed so confusing. How did people keep them straight? What made one color pretty and another ugly? This time I refused to be an outsider in a color-coded world. I had to ask.

"What did that shade of green look like?"

joy

Deana thought for a moment. "You know how it feels when you step in a lake and your foot hits a pile of mud—I mean gross, slimy mud that oozes between your toes?"

I could almost feel the slime between my toes. Ick. "Yeah."

"That's what the glass looked like. It wasn't rich forest green or pretty seafoam green. It was slimy-puke green."

"Eww. Good thing you told me before I proudly presented one to everyone in our room."

Nobody had ever described a color to me that way before. For once I felt a connection with the rest of the world. I understood what a color felt like and suddenly had an idea what it looked like. Okay, it was an ugly color, but still, I got it! I made a point to ask color questions more often.

Now my memory is full of moments when friends tried to describe colors to me in creative ways. Sometimes the descriptions were funny, like Deana's. Others were sweet and well thought out.

"Blue is like a cool breeze, or a clear sky."

"Red is like strawberries and brown is like chocolate.

"Orange is warm like the sun."

When people take the time to help me understand, not only do I appreciate colors more, but I am also reminded of an exciting reality. Someday I won't need an "interpreter"

debate

finals

ugly

green

puke

debate

finals

ugly

green

puke

anymore. I'll see every detail that I have ever missed on earth, including colors. Better yet, I'll see an untainted, perfected version of everything. There will be no slime green! Every shade and hue will be glorious.

My low vision may be a pain sometimes now, but it gives me all the more to look forward to in my eternal home. Not that I don't have enough to look forward to; when I really stop to think, I have a pretty long list.

I'll see my grandparents, and other loved ones who have gone on ahead of me.

Never again will I have to suffer through the evening news, worrying about terrorist attacks and wars. Fear will be a thing of the past.

I won't struggle with discouragement, depression, jealousy, or pride.

There will be no more concern about the uncertain future, or what my goals should be based on, or what I really want to do with my life.

I won't need makeup anymore, and there will be no more bad hair days!

Best of all, I'll finally meet Jesus.

As my mental list grows, so does my excitement. The idea of leaving this world for another one used to send me into a panic. I guess I don't like change. Now, as life gets more complicated and the world grows scarier by the day, I see how wonderful that change will be. Instead of letting the pain and uncertainty of living drag my spirit down, I can look up, knowing that something better is coming. As a believer in Jesus Christ, heaven is more than wishful thinking; it's reality.

No matter how bad life seems, I always have something to look forward to. I'm reminded every time I ask, "What does that color look like?"

a special prayer

Wonderful Creator, thank you for the promise of heaven. I can hardly wait to be transformed! Remind me more often of all that awaits me. Let the struggles of life fill me with a longing for Your kingdom and the moment when I will see You face to face. Amen.

questions:

Often we get so caught up in life, here on earth, that we forget something better awaits us. How excited are you, right now, about your eternal future?

❑ I can hardly wait.
❑ Pretty exciting, but life on earth is fun too.
❑ Thinking about heaven scares me. (Describe why.) (Lines)
❑ I don't really think about it much.

What things on earth remind you of heaven?

....

....

....

....

What are you most looking forward to in eternity?

....

....

....

....

What physical weaknesses or "character flaws" are you eager to shed?

. . . .

. . . .

. . . .

What about negative emotions and attitudes?

. . . .

. . . .

. . . .

Who are you looking forward to seeing?

. . . .

. . . .

. . . .

Write about a time when thinking about heaven lifted your spirits.

. . . .

. . . .

. . . .

. . . .

. . . .

. . . .

dig deeper

Read 1 Corinthians 2:9-10.

Describe what you think heaven will be like.

. . . .

. . . .

. . . .

. . . .

. . . .

In what ways do you think Hollywood and the media have warped our image of heaven? . . . .

. . . .

. . . .

. . . .

Read Revelation 21:3-4 and put yourself in the scene.
When God wipes tears from your eyes, what will those tears be for?

. . . .

. . . .

. . . .

. . . .

E veryone in our neighborhood knew "the lady with the walker." She stood outside her house almost every day, waving at people as they drove by and greeting kids as we walked home from school.

She had a thick German accent, and wore clunky shoes and frumpy dresses, but nobody dared make fun of her. Even a group of middle school boys occasionally stopped to talk to her.

I looked forward to passing this lady's street on my way home from the bus stop after a long day of classes.

"Hello!" she called one afternoon.

"Hi." I stopped and waved from across the street. "How are you?"

"I am fine." She announced, "It's my birthday. I'm 90 and I feel vonderful!"

"That's great." A smile escaped even though I'd had a crummy day. "Happy Birthday."

"Thank you, my darling."

I almost wished I'd known about her birthday earlier, so I could give her a card or something. Of course, it would have helped if I also knew her name.

The Lady with the Walker

How many people's lives had she saved?

One day I found out that the lady with the walker had received a humanitarian award, for hiding Jews in her house during the Holocaust. Suddenly she was more than just a cute, friendly old woman who waved at everyone she saw. She had a past (a heroic past. How many people's lives had she saved? How many times had she almost been caught? How often did she think about those families, huddled in her home so many years ago?

It gave me a much deeper appreciation for her daily

joy

"Hello, my darling!"

I often wondered, what kept her so vibrant and happy? Apparently, she lived with her son, but spent most of the day alone. Considering her history, she had endured more than her fair share of suffering. Even now, she relied on a walker to get around, and she obviously couldn't afford nice clothes. And on top of everything else, she was 90 years old. No way could she feel "vonderful" all the time. Still she ventured out, as often as she could, to wave and smile at passers-by, even if they didn't stop to notice.

What kept her going? I've decided that it was her willingness to leave that lonely house. She couldn't perform heroic deeds anymore, but she could still reach out. She could walk, wave, smile, and say, "Hello."

Instead of sitting in front of the television, gossiping on the phone, or moping around feeling sorry for herself, she enjoyed the fresh air and sunshine. Instead of dwelling on the past or whining about her dwindling energy, she charged forward in her rickety walker and used the energy she did have. Rather than grieving over the fact that she didn't have any friends around to keep her company, she made friends with her entire community, even though half of us never took the time to learn her name.

stood

waving

frumpy

heroic

lonely

stood

waving

frumpy

heroic

lonely

I also noticed that she never complained to those who stopped to chat with her. She talked about the good things in her life—the fact that she had 90 years to her credit and still felt great. She commented on what a beautiful day it was or "how pretty you look."

Her positive attitude made people love her. She lifted up everyone who passed her house. At the same time, it kept her spirits lifted.

When I'm 90, I hope that I'll be like the lady with the walker. No, I don't plan to stand on street corners, waving at strangers. But I do want to be known for a joyful heart and love for other people.

Proverbs 15:13,15 remind me that it all starts on the inside: "A joyful heart makes a cheerful face, but when the heart is sad, the spirit is broken. . . . All the days of the afflicted are bad, but a cheerful heart has a continual feast" (NASB).

A joyful heart isn't something I can force. I've learned the hard way that I can't fake it either. But the lady with the walker taught me that even when I'm at my lowest, a joyful heart is within my grasp if I really want it.

Sometimes it takes calling on God: "Heavenly Father, help me out of this bad mood. Give me something to smile about so I can shine for You."

The best thing that I can do when I am feeling down is get my mind off myself and turn it to someone else, like that sweet woman did each afternoon. Who needs cheering up? If I go for a walk, how many people can I smile at? Which of my friends needs a phone call or an encouraging note? Before I know it, my heart is lightened and I can sincerely reflect a cheerful spirit.

A special prayer

Lord, sometimes life is just tough. Still, I want to shine for You—to be a light in a dark world. Set my mind on others, God, instead of myself. Show me who needs a touch from You, through me. Give a cheerful heart, no matter what today brings. Amen.

questions:

Who is the most upbeat person you know? What do you think keeps him/her that way?.......................................
....
....

How do you feel when you are around a negative person, one who always talks about her own problems? ....
....
....

What about when you are around a cheerful person? ....
....
....
....

When you are down, what lifts you back up? ....
....
....
....
....

joy

Reflect on a time when reaching out to someone else helped you out of a bad mood. Write about the experience. . . . .
. . . .
. . . .
. . . .
. . . .
. . . .

dig deeper

Look through the book of Proverbs. List as many verses as you can find that talk about the benefits of a positive attitude or a cheerful heart. . . . .
. . . .
. . . .
. . . .
. . . .

Choose your favorite, write it down, and try memorizing it this week. . . . .
. . . .
. . . .
. . . .
. . . .
. . . .

How can you apply 1 Thessalonians 5:11 today?
. . . .
. . . .
. . . .
. . . .

Out of Place

I conned my parents

I'd never been invited to a party like Justin's before—one of those "Mom and Dad are out of town" colossal events that looked so fun in movies. And Justin invited me, the quiet, conservative one.

I had a huge crush on Justin. We'd performed a scene together in drama class that included a kiss and I'd been in love ever since. Sure I knew that Justin and his friends liked to drink—a lot. But so what? That didn't mean I had to.

Leaving out a few details about the party (the part about Justin's parents being gone, the strong possibility of underage drinking—little things like that), I conned my parents into letting me go. My sister and her boyfriend dropped me off.

"We'll pick you up in two hours," they promised.

I felt so ready to party in my trendy outfit. For a change, my hair and makeup both looked great. Justin greeted me at the door. Of course I melted. Maybe later we could re-enact our scene from drama class!

Instead, a half hour after my drop-off, I stood in the middle of Justin's living room, praying that my sister would show up early. If only she'd left a number where I could reach her. Everyone in the house was either drunk or on the way there. The house reeked of beer. Couples made out on couches and in corners. Whispers of drugs upstairs sent waves of dread through me.

I tried to talk to kids who walked by, but they all stared at me, as if I were some kind of alien in their midst, like they were wondering, "Who invited her?"

"Hey, Jeanette," Justin slurred on his way to the back deck, home of the ice chests and keg. "Having fun?"

"Yeah," I fibbed.

He squeezed my shoulder. I waited for that familiar "Justin touched me" thrill. Maybe it was the beer breath that killed it for me.

I looked at my watch for the hundredth time. A perfectly good Saturday night wasted.

Several hours later I lay in bed at home, beating myself up. Why hadn't I made more of an effort to have a good time? I could have asked Justin for a soda, or filled a cup with water, and found someone to talk to. Why did I just stand there, looking stupid? Would I ever learn to loosen up? Why couldn't I try to fit in? No wonder I never had any fun on the weekends.

Memories of that party haunted me for weeks. I felt embarrassed whenever I saw Justin in class.

Then one night, the light switch clicked on. No, I didn't have one of those "I opened my Bible to Ephesians and . . ." moments. God simply whispered to my heart. As a Christian, I didn't fit in at a party like Justin's, with drinking, no parents and rumors of drugs. I had no business drooling over a guy who spent most Sunday mornings recovering from a hangover.

Never mind the fact that getting to the party required lying to Mom and Dad. I had a crummy time, not because I didn't know how to have fun or refused to mix, but because I didn't

quiet

crush

trendy

drunk

dread

quiet

crush

trendy

drunk

dread

mix. God never wanted me at Justin's house. Even the other guests knew I was in the wrong place.

This wasn't the first time that I had tried to take a step over to the wild side, thinking kids had more fun over there than in my G-rated world. When would I get the clue? It always turned out the same—with some form of guilt, regrets, and the horrible feeling of not belonging.

If I wanted to enjoy my Saturday nights, or anything else, then maybe I needed to spend time in an activity that lined up with God's desire for me. If I wanted to stop feeling out of place all the time, I needed to find a crowd that I actually belonged in—like a group of Christians.

No more parties like Justin's, I decided. I knew this would mean letting go of some friendships, including his. I could forget about ever being accepted by his group. But suddenly I didn't care. In fact, it felt really good knowing that God had something better in mind for me, His child. He would send me friends, real friends. So what if I never lost my reputation as the quiet, conservative one.

That's how God made me. He had called me to live differently—to stand out for Him—and I was finally ready to obey. Maybe Justin's party hadn't been such a wasted Saturday night after all.

A special prayer

Father, give me courage to turn down invitations that will lead me where I don't belong. Thank You for those moments of misery that put me back on track. Use them as sober reminders of Your mercy. Increase my desire to have fun in ways that please You. Amen.

questions:

How do you feel when you are in a place where you know God doesn't want you? ....
. . . .
. . . .
. . . .

Compare that with the joy of doing His will. . . . .
. . . .
. . . .
. . . .

When have you lied or left out details in order to get Mom and Dad's permission to do something? . . . .
. . . .
. . . .
. . . .

What were the consequences? . . . .
. . . .
. . . .
. . . .
. . . .

As we grow in faith, our taste in entertainment, friendships, and use of free time tends to change. How has your taste changed for the better?

. . . .

. . . .

. . . .

What benefits have you found in spending time with other believers as opposed to those who don't share your values?

. . . .

. . . .

. . . .

. . . .

. . . .

. . . .

dig deeper

Read 1 Peter 1:13-17.

When has it been hard for you to obey God? . . . .

. . . .

. . . .

What difference do you see in your attitude and outlook toward life when you choose to live the way He wants you to? . . . .

. . . .

. . . .

. . . .

. . . .

Read Philippians 3:7-9.

Paul gave up a lot to follow Christ. Yet it all seemed like garbage compared to the greatness of serving his Lord.

What activities, relationships, or dreams did you leave behind when you decided to live for Jesus? *joy*

. . . .

. . . .

. . . .

. . . .

. . . .

How has God blessed your life since? . . . .

. . . .

. . . .

. . . .

. . . .

. . . .

. . . .

Storms

"Storm 2005" was the biggest that Reno, Nevada, had seen since 1911. In two weeks, the sky dumped three feet of snow in a city that usually measured its snow in inches.

Nicole's family had never seen such horrible weather.

"We're going to die from the cold," Nicole said through chattering teeth. "Like the Donner Party. Who should we eat first?"

"Before we eat anyone, we need to clear the driveway again," her dad grumbled.

Nicole shivered when she looked out at the knee-deep snow that she was sure to spend the next two hours trudging through. Icicles hung from the roof, many so long they resembled swords from an ice-age fantasy film. At first the snow had been fun—especially when school got cancelled for three days. Now it was just a pain.

As soon as she got outside with shovel in hand, she saw Roger Milton, her friend Sammy's dad, making his way across the unplowed street. He carried two heavy-duty snow shovels—much better than the cheap plastic shovels that Nicole's family had been working with all week.

"Let me give you a hand," Mr. Milton shouted.

The Miltons had just moved to Reno from Maine—to escape the harsh New England winters. They spent the next week passing their blizzard-survival skills on to Nicole's family.

Sammy gave Nicole a lesson on how to drive over snow and ice so she wouldn't be the next student at Reno High to get into an accident.

Sammy's parents went from house to house, helping people with their driveways and sidewalks. They gave lessons on how to knock icicles down without damaging the roof or getting hit in the head, and how to deice walkways. Mrs. Milton took Nicole's mom

Like the
Donner Party

joy

shopping for better winter clothes for the family. She even shared her secret recipe for hot chocolate.

One Saturday morning, while shoveling snow from the third and last storm, Nicole stopped to catch her breath. She turned to Sammy. "Well, if my dad ever gets transferred to North Dakota or something, at least we'll know how to survive the winter."

"Or if this happens again in Reno, you'll be able to help someone else."

"Right now my plan is to move to Hawaii after graduation."

* * *

The storms of life are rarely fun. Bad weather is bad enough. But what about life-storms—the heartbreaks, losses, and disappointments? It feels like the bitter cold will never end. Your heart will always ache. You'll cry yourself to sleep every night for the rest of your life. What a gift it is when God sends someone your way who has been through the same thing and can help you get through the blizzard.

When my first boyfriend broke up with me, I thought my heart would break down the middle. Who were the first friends to give me the sympathy I needed? Those who already knew the excruciating pain of lost love.

A couple of years later, when I started feeling depressed, something prompted me to tell my singing teacher. As it turned out, she once battled depression. She listened and encouraged

snow

die

pain

harsh

survive

snow

die

pain

harsh

survive

me. Later she referred me to a great Christian counselor. It helped so much to have living proof that the darkness would not last forever. Talking to her erased my fears that I wasn't praying enough, that I didn't trust God, or that I was crazy.

When I decided that the best way to lose weight was to starve myself, I wasn't so fortunate. I didn't have a friend who had gone through the same struggle. Looking back, recovery might have been much easier if I went through it with someone who "got it."

Still, that experience equipped me to support and help a friend when I found out she had a similar problem.

I can honestly say I praise God for many stormy periods of my life. How can I not, when I see how He has used each one? My relationship with God has been taken to new depths, along with my appreciation for whoever helped me through each trial. After I get through a crisis, I can help someone else through hers. I have a better idea of what to say and do when someone aches from loss, depression, or a desire to damage her body—thanks to great compassion for the pain they are going through. Like my voice teacher was for me, I am able to stand as living proof that the storms do end eventually.

So I guess I should learn to say, "God, bring on the storms."

a special prayer

Father, may I never forget what if feels like to hurt or struggle. Thank You for friends that You sent my way, just when I needed them. I thank You that the storms of life don't come from a cruel-hearted God, but from One who allows everything for my good. Amen.

questions:

List three people who have helped you through a difficult time in your life...
....
....

What did each person help you through? ....
....
....
....
....

Write about a time when you didn't have someone who had been there to help you during difficult days. How did you get through it? ....
....
....
....

How have the trials and difficulties of life equipped you to support others?
....
....
....
....
....
....

Write about a specific time. . . . .

joy

. . . .

. . . .

. . . .

. . . .

. . . .

How have experiences with helping others, through trials that you experienced
yourself, helped you to grow? . . . .

. . . .

. . . .

. . . .

dig deeper

How does 2 Corinthians 1:3-5 encourage you in any trial you are dealing with
right now? . . . .

. . . .

. . . .

. . . .

When you are struggling and don't know of anyone who understands what you are
dealing with, how can Hebrews 2:17-18 encourage you? . . . .

. . . .

. . . .

. . . .

. . . .

. . . .

What's On Your Mind?

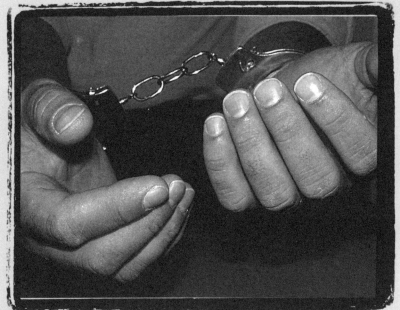

I found myself constantly worrying

What did you fall asleep thinking about last night?

. . . .
. . . .
. . . .

What thought woke you up in the middle of the night or kept you from sleeping?

. . . .
. . . .
. . . .

What was the first thing that came to mind when you woke up?

. . . .
. . . .
. . . .

Lately, if you catch your brain wandering in class, where does it go?

. . . .
. . . .
. . . .

In some ways, our thoughts are like cats: Sometimes they're hard to hold onto, while other times they won't leave us alone.

I have always had to keep close tabs on my thought life. Shortly after the 9/11 terrorist attacks,

I found myself constantly worrying about world events. It didn't help that the news constantly bombarded me with horrible possibilities:

"If a terrorist attack took place in your city, how would you respond?" What if that did happen?

"Does your family have a disaster plan?" Did we?

"War is imminent." What if they invade us first?

I tossed and turned by night, and by day walked around with my stomach in triple knots. One afternoon I went to my friend Susan's house and poured out my fears. Tears came quickly as I confessed, "I'm so tired of being afraid all the time."

To her, the answer was simple. "Stop thinking about it."

Stop thinking about it? How can I just shut off all the bad thoughts?

"Do something to get your mind off all this stuff. It's not like we have any control over it. Stop watching the news if you have to."

Avoiding the news seemed like a good place to start. When somebody turned on the TV news, I left the room and focused on something more pleasant. It took awhile, but the more I practiced shifting my thoughts to things other than death and the uncertain future, the more I felt my fear diminish.

Once our country went to war, I had to start all over again. I would hear stories of evil men

asleep

mind

go

war

worry

asleep

mind

go

war

worry

killing or torturing entire families and think, What if that happened to me? Terrifying images filled my mind. The more I dwelled on them, the more anxious and depressed I became.

I tried to focus on reassuring thoughts that tried to break through: That isn't happening to you, so stop tormenting yourself. Remember Susan's advice. Think about something good.

Yet quickly my thoughts would again become my worst enemy.

I've lost sleep over less tragic problems too. If a friend says something to hurt or irritate me, I can't let it go. I replay the scene in my head more times than I need to, rehearse what I would say if I had the guts, and let my anger boil. By morning I wonder why my offender and I are even friends.

Or I make a mistake and can't get it out of my head. My mind spins with "should haves" and "what ifs." Before I know it, I didn't just mess up; I'm a horrible person.

Can you relate at all?

When I recognize how destructive my own thoughts can be, I understand why Paul took a few moments to address the subject while writing to his friends in Philippi. He knew that they had a lot to worry about—persecution and invasion, as well as the typical daily concerns of living and growing in the Christian faith. They could easily become discouraged, maybe even give up, if they didn't keep their list of concerns in check and focus instead on God's goodness.

At the time of his writing, Paul was in prison chained to guards, with no privacy and no release dates in sight. Already he had suffered unimaginable physical abuse. Friends had abandoned him. Chances are he had learned that the things he filled his mind with had the power to make or break his day. He could let himself fall into an abyss of despair over the unfairness of it all, getting mad at God and complaining, "Hey, I chose to serve You and this is what I get?" Or he could consider the glorious hope he had ahead—no matter what happened—and the remarkable changes that had taken place in his life, and the power of the gospel he saw all around him.

When I read that famous passage, "Finally, brethren, whatever is true, whatever is honorable, . . ." I have to say to myself, "If Paul can do it, then I can certainly give it a try." Sometimes I like to flip the order of Philippians 4:8 and 4:7 around: "And the peace of God, which surpasses all comprehension, will guard your hearts and your minds in Christ Jesus" (NASB). When my mind is focused on Him and the things that please Him, I go from troubled and anxious to filled with His peace.

a special prayer

Father, I can't control the ups and downs of life. What I choose to dwell on, though, is my choice. The world is a frightening place, but You are so good. Fill my heart and mind with reminders of Your faithfulness or love. Let my thinking be centered on You today. Amen.

question:

Chances are you have some concerns right now. List those that you can't help dwelling on.........................

. . . .

. . . .

. . . .

. . . .

. . . .

Which of the following issues do you find yourself worrying about often?

❑ Wars, natural disasters, and other world events

❑ Your future

❑ Your looks and/or weight

❑ Family problems

❑ A recent fight with a friend

❑ Problems with your boyfriend

❑ Your salvation

❑ Something else . . . .
. . . .

Ask God to give you peace about these concerns and to help you focus on more productive things.

Remember the last time you had a really bad day. How much of it had to do with your thinking instead of your circumstances? . . . .
. . . .

Our spiritual lives and our thought lives tend to be closely related. What steps do you need to take in the areas of prayer, Bible study, and time alone with God in order to get your mind on the right track? . . . .
. . . .
. . . .
. . . .

dig deeper

Read Philippians 4:8. Take some time to let the words sink in, even if you've read this verse 500 times.
List some pure, lovely, and praiseworthy thoughts that you can dwell on today. . . . .
. . . .
. . . .

If you find your head is full of thoughts you know to be lies, what truth can you replace them with? . . . .
. . . .
. . . .
. . . .

Backtrack to verse 7. Why does our ability to experience the peace of God have so much to do with our thoughts? . . . .
. . . .
. . . .
. . . .

Look up Psalm 104:33-34 and read it as if it were your own prayer. How can you shift your thinking so it is more pleasing to God? . . . .
. . . .
. . . .
. . . .

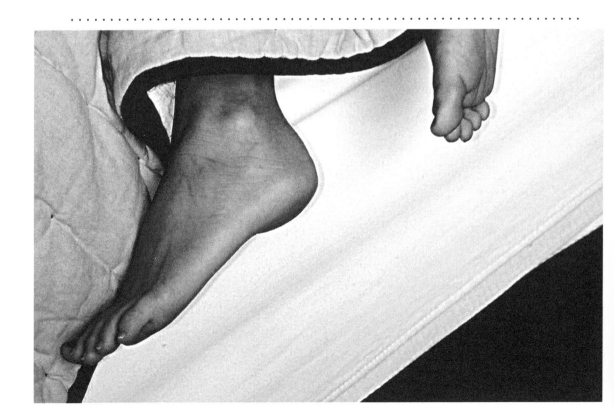

I really wanted my friend Tori to accept Christ. Having Him to turn to might make her tough home life easier to deal with. Plus, if the Rapture took place tomorrow, I didn't want her left behind.

Pressure's Off

I came right out and asked

One afternoon we started talking about God on our way home from school. I must admit, I sort of manipulated the conversation in that direction.

I started out by inviting Tori to church. She turned me down.

Then, surprised by my own boldness, I came right out and asked, "Are you a Christian?" knowing the answer.

"Probably. I believe in God."

I tried to think of a super spiritual response that would immediately open Tori's eyes to her need for a personal relationship with God through Jesus.

I'd had very little practice sharing Christ. I envied the uninhibited Christian kids I knew. Leslie for example, carried her Bible to school and could quote all the best witnessing Scriptures from memory. She wasn't afraid to use words like sin and hell. Okay, Leslie wasn't exactly the most popular girl on campus, but she did know how to speak the truth. What would she say to Tori?

I cleared my throat. "Actually, you need to ask Jesus to forgive your sins and accept Him as your savior to be a Christian."

"That's not true," Tori snapped.

Everything I said after that came out wrong. It didn't help that, unlike me, Tori loved to argue and had a rebuttal for everything. When I tried to scare her with the possibility of not going to heaven, she questioned why a loving God would send a good person anywhere else. When I started to back up one of my points with, "Well, the Bible says . . ." she told me that the Bible is just a book of stories. By the time we reached my house, Tori was treating me like an ignorant fanatic, and I felt like a faith-sharing failure.

For the next hour I racked my brain for ideas about how to fix the situation, to mend my friendship with Tori and get her to accept Jesus at the same time. I spotted some back issues of Mom's favorite devotional guide. One pocket-sized booklet had the title Jesus Is Coming Soon: Will You Be Ready? Ooh, perfect! Tori might listen to a well-known evangelist.

"Can I have this?" I asked Mom.

She glanced at the book. "Sure."

I stuffed it into my pocket along with another old issue that had a catchy title. "I'll be right back."

I headed to Tori's house. When she answered the door, I handed her the booklets. "Maybe these will help you understand what I was talking about."

I stood motionless, waiting for her to invite me in or say, "On second thought, I will go to church with you this Sunday." Instead she looked at the books, rolled her eyes, and took a

tough

rapture

truth

scare

peace

tough

rapture

truth

scare

peace

step backward. "Thanks. See you tomorrow."

"Bye." I should say something else, something better. But what? My mind went blank, paralyzed by Tori's stubbornness. I had blown it again.

But as I dragged my feet home, I sensed God whispering to my heart, You did your part.

Did I? What else could I say or do? Nothing really. Any more might push Tori further away. She had heard the Truth and held a tool in her hand that could answer some of her questions. The rest was between Tori and God.

I never stopped praying for Tori. To this day I don't know where she stands with God, or if she even cracked the covers of those booklets. But I have peace, knowing that her salvation is in God's hands and that I did my part in pointing her to the Savior.

The whole process of sharing my faith intimidates me. It got easier when I accepted that God never asked me to be like Leslie—scaring people into repenting.

I've learned that I'm much more effective when I speak from my heart, share how Christ has changed my life, and let my love for Him flow out naturally. Sometimes the best way for me to share Jesus is to reach out with a touch from Him—to listen, hug someone who is hurting, offer to pray. That alone opens door.

As much as I long to see everyone that I care

about come to Jesus, I am grateful that each one's salvation is not up to me. It takes the pressure out of witnessing and turns it into an exciting experience of offering hope to someone who needs it. When I get to heaven, I may discover that my words had greater power than I thought. Until then, I pray I will stay open to any opportunities God provides for me to share about His Son.

a special prayer

Lord, it breaks my heart to think of those around me who don't know You. Give me the gentle spirit I need to share the way of salvation. Help me leave the results up to You. Work in the hearts of friends I have shared You with already. Amen

questions:

List some people whose salvation you are praying for
. . . .
. . . .
. . . .

What is your typical reaction when you have an opportunity to share about Christ?
. . . .
. . . .

How do you respond if that person rejects what you have to say?
. . . .
. . . .
. . . .

In what ways do you think your attitude and choices witness to nonbelievers?
. . . .
. . . .
. . . .
. . . .

Why do you think it is so tempting to beat nonbelievers over the head with the truth of the Gospel? . . . .

. . . .

Why is it so difficult to leave the results in God's hands? . . . .

. . . .

. . . .

dig deeper

Read Acts 26:1-18, 28-29.
Why do you think Paul's testimony had such power? . . . .

. . . .

. . . .

. . . .

Why do you think the stories of God's work in individual lives are so often more effective than quoting Bible verses and tracts? . . . .

. . . .

. . . .

. . . .

Read 1 Corinthians 3:5-9.
How does this passage put your heart at ease when it comes to telling others about Christ? . . . .

. . . .

. . . .

What seeds of faith might you have planted recently? . . . .

. . . .

. . . .

. . . .

. . . .

List these people by name so you can remember to pray for them. . . . .

joy

. . . .

. . . .

. . . .

. . . .

How does this passage encourage you to reach out even more? . . . .

. . . .

. . . .

. . . .

How does understanding God's role in the salvation process, compared to your own role, change the way you look at sharing your faith? . . . .

. . . .

. . . .

. . . .

. . . .

Someone Who Hears

the gateway to a one-on-one relation-ship with an awesome God

"I don't think God hears my prayers." Alicia's heartache and words broke my heart. I didn't know what to say. She had just gotten some bad news and was deeply upset.

I'd tried my best to comfort her over the phone. "I'll pray for you," I promised before we hung up. Then she blurted it out: God didn't hear her prayers.

The truth was, I didn't know if God acknowledged Alicia's prayers or not. Sure God probably heard them. He saw and heard everything. But would He listen and respond to Alicia? She wasn't a Christian. To her, prayer was something that a person did when she was in trouble or needed something. Prayer was not the gateway to a one-on-one relationship with an awesome God.

I had talked to her about God many times. Alicia seemed to want some spirituality in her life, but she had no desire to become "religious." Now, while she was hurting, probably wouldn't be a good time to point out, "God isn't a magic genie, Alicia. You need a relationship with Him."

So I fumbled through a while longer, trying to give Alicia hope, and hung up feeling like I had said all the wrong things.

I had no idea what it felt like to wonder whether or not God heard me when I prayed. I'd gone through times of questioning what He was doing or if He cared. I'll admit I've been mad at Him a few times.

But I grew up in a home where God was always part

of life. Mom and Dad led me to accept Jesus as my Savior at age five. I couldn't remember a day when I didn't know He was up there seeing and hearing me. Even during those years when I didn't attend church or walk closely with God, I knew He hadn't gone anywhere. If I wanted to talk to Him, He would listen.

"God, I wish Alicia knew You, so she could cry out to You and know that You hear her."

I prayed a lot for Alicia and her many problems. The more I prayed and remembered the wall that existed between her and God, the more grateful I felt for the fact that I could pray and be heard by the Lord of the universe: "I love the Lord, because He hears my voice and my supplications" (Psalm 116:1 NASB).

What an awesome reality!

No matter what I'm going through, no matter how deep my pain, anger, or confusion, God knows and wants me to run to Him with all of it—to burst into His throne room at anytime and cry, "Father, help!" When I am excited or thankful, He wants me to share those emotions too. Unlike Alicia, I am never without a friend to listen, even to my most private prayers.

Before that conversation with Alicia, I never thought of prayer as something I could take for granted. Since birth I have been told, "Say your prayers." "Pray about it." "We need to pray for . . ." It's routine.

I've watched movies and television shows

broke

blurted

trouble

magic

love

broke

blurted

trouble

magic

love

joy

where anyone in a crisis can say through tears, "God, if you're up there . . .well . . . I'm not the praying type but . . . "I'm in a mess" and receive instant help. It's easy to forget that prayer is a privilege for those who know God.

Prayer is one of God's greatest gifts to His children. Yet how often do I fail to go to God first? Or to call on Him when I need to? I run to Him after I've tried to reach my friends. I save the major crisis for Him and choose to handle the everyday struggles on my own. Other times I whip through a quick prayer as if it were nothing more than another item on my to-do list.

Brush teeth—check.

Make bed—yep, did that.

Oh yeah, I should probably pray.

Let's see. I have two minutes.

Unless I'm going through an especially difficult time, or praising Him for something big, I often fail to appreciate the incredible truth that the God who created me is listening intently to every word I say or think. I know it, but is it as big a deal to me as it should be? Does the knowledge of communicating with the only God Who listens to His faithful ones fill me with the wonder and reverence that it should? You'd think I'd want to talk to Him all the time, about everything! And what a change takes place in me when I do go to Him more often.

How different would my life be if each day was a continual conversation with God?

a special prayer

Lord, thank You that I can call on You and that You eagerly listen to me.. You not only hear and care, but You really want to communicate with me. Forgive the times when I've neglected my prayer life, or thought of it too casually. May today be a constant conversation with You. Amen.

a prayer of thanks

Write your own expression of thanks to God for a special time of prayer that you had recently, or a prayer that you are particularly grateful to know God heard.

. . . .

. . . .

. . . .

. . . .

. . . .

questions:

How do you know that God hears your prayers? . . . .
. . . .
. . . .
. . . .

What role does prayer have in your family's life? . . . .
. . . .
. . . .

When do you usually pray the hardest? . . . .
. . . .
. . . .
. . . .

How does knowing that God hears your prayers change your response to problems? . . . .

. . . .

. . . .

dig deeper

How does the truth in Hebrews 4:14-16 make it easier to approach God honestly in your prayers? . . . .

. . . .

. . . .

Read Psalm 5:1-2, 7-8, 11-12.

What do you need God's help with right now? Or what direction do you need from Him? . . . .

. . . .

. . . .

. . . .

What do these verses tell you about the privilege of prayer?

. . . .

. . . .

How has God protected or blessed you recently?

. . . .

. . . .

. . . .

Pray for someone who doubts God's ability to hear prayers. If this person does not have a relationship with God, add a prayer for his or her salvation.

. . . .

. . . .

. . . .

What My Father Remembers

no flaws, no days of
rebellion to regret, and
no mistakes

At my sister Kristy's wedding, Dad made everyone cry with his speech about what it was like to have Kristy as a daughter. He didn't talk about the time she almost burned the house down, the tantrums she threw as a toddler, or the times that he had to discipline her. As far as anyone at the wedding knew, Kristy brought nothing but joy to her parents.

With teary eyes, we all laughed as Dad shared stories from Kristy's preteen tomboy years. While Sherry and I played with Barbie dolls in the house, Kristy played football with the boys at the park and won a spot on the all-stars softball team.

"She always had her blond curls pulled back into neat ponytails, with bows or ponytail holders to match her softball uniform," Dad reminded us. Kristy's softball photo flashed through my mind. She could have won the award for most color coordinated.

He talked about her growing up into a teenager who suddenly wouldn't go fishing with Dad, unless she had her makeup on and the perfect outfit, complete with accessories.

Dad told about the day that Kristy brought Ian (the man she was marrying) home to meet him and Mom for the first time.

He wrapped up his speech with a sweet expression of how much he loved watching

Kristy grow up and how much he would miss having her at home. That day Kristy had no flaws, no days of rebellion to regret, and no mistakes to fear having revealed in public. Dad remembered only the good stuff.

It hit me recently that this is how my heavenly Father sees me. The day I accepted Christ as my Savior, every lie, moment of disobedience, and bad decision got wiped from the slate. God chose to forget it all—to put it behind Him forever. To Him, I am His precious, blameless child. I don't need to fear getting to heaven, only to have Father break out the video of my most sinful moments. Like Dad on Kristy's wedding day, my heavenly Father remembers only the good.

When I think of all God could hold against me—how often I have failed Him, even as a Christian, even when I knew better—I am humbled and amazed. I would sure still be angry with me for some of those poor choices. Yet, He tells me, "I have swept away your offenses like a cloud, your sins like the morning mist. . . . Sing for joy, O heavens, for the Lord has

burned

tantrum

cry

neat

perfect

burned

tantrum

cry

neat

perfect

done this" (Isaiah 44:22-23).

No matter how offensive my behavior is to God, all I need to do is admit, "God, I completely blew it, please forgive me," and it's done. It almost seems too easy.

Maybe that's why I have a hard time accepting forgiveness sometimes. I don't have much trouble admitting when I've done something wrong. My problem is that, with certain mistakes, I beat myself up long after my confession. I don't deserve to have that sin forgiven and forgotten. I've had people in my life tell me, "I forgive you," only to hold that mistake against me when I least expect it. Why shouldn't my perfect God do the same?

I guess that's exactly what makes God's mercy so incredible. He forgives when I deserve a public trial and execution. He forgets when He has every right to say repeatedly, "Now Jeanette, remember the time when you. . . . How do I know you won]t go out and do the same thing again?"

That's why Jesus came, I must constantly remember, to die for all sins, past, present, and future. God assures me of that through

Jesus' own words in Matthew 26:28: "This is my blood of the covenant, which is poured out for many for the forgiveness of sins." Acts 3:19 reminds me, "Repent, then, and turn to God, so that your sins may be wiped out, that times of refreshing may come from the Lord."

So instead of living in the shadows of my regrets, I can accept God's forgiveness and His cleansing with inexpressible gratitude and experience the joy that comes when I do. Why try to make sense of something I will never understand? Why waste time dwelling on every mistake I've made since . . .well . . .as long as I can remember, when I can put them behind me and move on as God does?

I think it's time to spend more time thinking about what my Heavenly Father remembers—the good He has accomplished in me, despite all my imperfections.

a special prayer

Heavenly Father, when I think of all the times I've failed and disobeyed You, I am overwhelmed by Your ability to forgive and forget. Let me never take advantage of such a gift. Lift the heaviness of sin from my heart and replace it with gratitude for Your cleansing power.

questions:

List some mistakes that God has forgiven you for recently. Which ones are you most thankful to know He has wiped from the slate? . . . .

. . . .

. . . .

. . . .

. . . .

How does knowing that you have confessed a sin and been forgiven affect your outlook on life? . . . .

. . . .

. . . .

. . . .

How does it affect your relationships with other people? . . . .

joy

. . . .

. . . .

. . . .

. . . .

Why do you think it is so difficult to forgive ourselves for some things, even when
we know God has forgiven us? . . . .

. . . .

. . . .

. . . .

Ask God to help you let go of a mistake that you still feel guilty for, even though
you know He has already cleansed you of it. Write the prayer out as a reminder.

. . . .

. . . .

. . . .

. . . .

. . . .

. . . .

dig deeper

Psalm 32 contrasts the power of guilt with the freedom of forgiveness.
Write about a time when you felt like David did in verses 3-4.

. . . .

. . . .

. . . .

What happened to you on the inside when you finally confessed?

. . . .

. . . .

. . . .

joy

What are the biggest blessings in being forgiven? . . . .

. . . .

. . . .

. . . .

Read Isaiah 43:18-19

Why do you think God discourages us from dwelling on the past? . . . .

. . . .

. . . .

. . . .

How can you use your past and all God has forgiven in your life to bring hope to someone else's future? . . . .

. . . .

. . . .

. . . .

. . . .

. . . .

Opening Night

they already
assumed I'd be
famous someday

Mom's friend Yolanda bounced down the steps of the high school theater. She threw her arms around me. "Oh, Jeanette, you were so good!"

Her husband Craig handed me his program. "Will you sign this?"

Yolanda dug through her purse for a pen. "When you're famous we can say, 'That's our Jeanette.'"

My first autograph—yes! And they already assumed I'd be famous someday. I started to picture myself starring in a movie, hanging out with my favorite actors and actresses, and knowing every kid who was ever mean to me wished they'd been nicer so they could say, "I know her. She's a friend of mine."

Mom and Dad stood back, wearing the typical proud-parent grins. My sisters actually looked happy to be related to me. From everyone's reaction and the way I felt inside, you'd think I'd had the lead. Actually, my character was only in Act II and spent most of it passed out on the couch. But hey, it was my first high school play, and I was still only a freshman. The best was yet to come.

It was official—I had found my place, my talent! Finally, after so many years of not being good at anything special—or at least not feeling good at anything. Now, when relatives or one of Mom and Dad's friends asked, "What are your hobbies?" I had an answer. I could proudly say, "Drama."

Of course the part hadn't dropped in my lap. First I had to audition, setting aside my fears of making a fool of myself or not getting a part. Instead of going for a major role, I played it safe and tried for something small but fun.

I didn't even mind giving up my afternoons for rehearsals. In fact, I loved saying, "I have rehearsal," knowing that I was part of something important.

Okay, practice wasn't always pleasant. Sometimes I left frustrated, because it seemed like I would never please our drama teacher with the way I said my lines or portrayed my character. But I was determined to do a good job, so I let Ms. Goodwin's critiques drive me to improve.

Now, on opening night, I saw the rewards of all the hard work and sacrifice. I also found a new version of joy—the joy of discovering and using a gift. I couldn't stop smiling. How many hours until tomorrow night's performance? Do we really have to wait until next year to do another play?

So far, drama hasn't made me famous, as Craig and Yolanda predicted. But I still thank God for every opportunity He has given me to perform. What could be more fun than doing something I both enjoy and feel I'm good at?

Since that first school play, I have won larger parts and branched out into singing and writing scripts. God has opened doors for me to use my skills to serve Him through church drama.

Some things haven't changed. Auditioning, performing, and writing still involve risk,

famous

actor

talent

small

risk

famous

actor

talent

small

risk

sacrifice, and hard work. I've had to learn to accept criticism and rejection along with the compliments. But in the end, the hard work pays off.

The best rewards come when I use these talents to serve God. No matter how small my part is, I can see it making a difference:

"That song really ministered to me."

"After the Easter play, seven people came forward to accept Christ."

I am reminded what using my gifts is really about. Better still, I sense that God is pleased.

When I read Jesus' Parable of the Talents, I can't help feeling sorry for that last servant, the one who buried his talent in the sand instead of investing it. He missed out on so much. Besides the obvious consequences of his master's severe response, he never experienced the thrill of putting his small gift to use and watching it grow beyond his expectations. He didn't get to see it have an impact in people's lives, including his own.

Worst of all, he lost what little he had, when he could have heard, "Well done," from the One who trusted him with the talent in the first place.

I continually pray that I will never waste my talents, even if they seem small and insignificant. I look forward to the day when I can lay each one at my Master's feet, and hear Him say, "Well done."

God, every good gift comes from You, including any abilities that *joy* I have. Thank You for opening so many doors for me to use them and for helping small talents to grow beyond my dreams. May I never grow tired of using my gifts to serve and glorify You. Amen.

questions:

Reflect on how it feels to do something that you know you are good at. Thank God for allowing your gifts and talents to be so fun..
. . . .

How have you seen your mood or focus change while using one of your talents?

. . . .
. . . .
. . . .

How often do you wish that God had gifted you in some other way, thinking that your gifts aren't useful enough? Read what Paul has to say in 1 Corinthians 12:14-27. Ask God to help you appreciate and enjoy the abilities that He has equipped you with. . . . .
. . . .
. . . .

Think of a friend or family member who is extremely talented, but either doesn't realize his or her giftedness or is afraid to pursue it. How can you encourage him or her to step out and try? . . . .
. . . .
. . . .
. . . .
. . . .

joy

Read Matthew 25:14-30.

In what ways has God gifted you creatively, athletically, or intellectually?

. . . .
. . . .
. . . .

How are you using these gifts? . . . .

. . . .
. . . .
. . . .

Think of a talent you know you have but are not making use of. What is keeping you from using it? Time? Money? . . . .

. . . .
. . . .

Ask God to open a door for you to use this gift.

What talents are you neglecting out of fear or (sometimes this one is hard to admit) laziness? . . . .

. . . .
. . . .

Read Romans 12:4-8.

What opportunities have you had to use your talents and interests to serve God?

. . . .
. . . .
. . . .
. . . .
. . . .

What rewards have come from those experiences? . . . .

joy

. . . .

. . . .

. . . .

. . . .

How does the joy of using your abilities for Him compare to using them for your own benefit or to please people? . . . .

. . . .

. . . .

. . . .

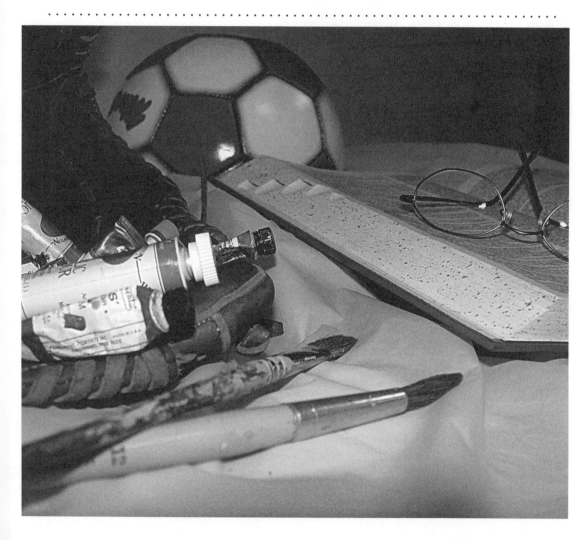

Letting Go

The college theater department was nothing like my high school drama club. Students saw cast parties as opportunities to get drunk. They talked openly about taking drugs and "sleeping together"—that kind of sleeping together.

Scenes my drama teacher assigned in class often contained language I'd never been allowed to mutter under my breath, let alone say "with conviction" to a room full of people. During a summer musical I got yelled at repeatedly for looking too stiff during a dance where I had to shimmy toward the audience.

"Come on, Jeanette, shake it!"

How could I ever feel comfortable "shaking it"? My parents would die of shock when they saw the play!

I tried to convince myself, "It's no big deal." I laughed off the shimmy scene with my family and kept other things I'd been exposed to quiet. If I was going to act, I needed to get used to these things, right? It's not like I planned to start condoning the choices that my friends from the drama club made. My family wasn't attending church at the time, so I guess my conviction level was running a little low.

I hid my shock and tried to go with the flow. Then something a little scary happened. I started enjoying the wild atmosphere, even if I didn't take part in the "bad stuff." I had a reputation as the pure, naive one. Everyone in the drama department thought it was so sweet that I'd never taken drugs, gotten drunk, or lost my virginity. And I didn't plan to anytime soon? Wow, how weird! I can't count how many times I heard, "Jeanette, you're so cute.

start condoning the choices

You're so . . .innocent."

Then my friend Robert invited me to church and I renewed my relationship with God. It hit me that I wouldn't feel comfortable inviting friends from church to a college play. Our director had a reputation for choosing shows that were, let's say, not exactly family friendly. What would my friends think if they read some of the scripts I'd rehearsed for class?

But I loved acting. Would God really ask me to give up my dream of pursuing it professionally? That didn't seem fair. Why give me desire and talent if He didn't want me to use them? What else could He possibly have for me that I loved as much?

Suddenly I felt lost, depressed, and confused.

So far I'd compromised only in little ways—language, subject matter, embarrassing dance moves. What would be next? How far would I be asked to go? Sure, the other drama students still knew me as the innocent one, so I obviously hadn't changed much. I stayed away from the parties now. But I was getting a little tired of being laughed at for my innocence. Now that I knew more Christians, I felt kind of proud of the fact that certain things still shocked me. But the dream of appearing on the Academy Awards wouldn't go away.

Certain questions kept coming to mind: Can

scenes
drama
mutter
shake
exposed
scenes
drama
mutter
shake
exposed

I pursue my dream and honor God? Is this where He wants me?

Finally I had to accept the answer—No. Maybe other Christian actors could do it, but God had other plans for me.

Many times after that I tried to turn back to acting. I would watch a play or a movie and feel that burning desire to go for it again. Occasionally I auditioned for local theater productions. Each time I heard, You did a great job!" but I never got a part. It took a long time for me to finally let go. Shortly after I did, I found a new acting opportunity in church drama.

Giving up my theater major was one of the hardest things that I ever had to do. But I don't regret it. God wasn't trying to cold-heartedly take away something I loved "because I'm God and being a Christian involves sacrifice." He knew that I was in danger of putting my dream above Him. And look what happened when I truly obeyed and stopped trying to change my mind. He gave what I enjoyed back to me in a different form. He also led me to a career that I love as much as acting, maybe even more. Better still, I am content, knowing what I do pleases the God I love.

Now if I watch the Oscars, I don't ache to appear at the podium. Instead, I say to myself, I don't think I would have been very happy in Hollywood. I wouldn't fit in very well.

Obviously God knew that. It just took me a while to accept it.

a special prayer

God, Your direction isn't always easy to follow. But the rewards of sacrificial obedience are worth the pain. Thank You for knowing what is best for me, even when I don't. Thanks for never taking without giving back. May I never put my dreams above Your desire for me. Amen.

questions:

List some of your plans and dreams for the future.
. . . .
. . . .
. . . .

How are you hoping to glorify God through them? . . . .
. . . .
. . . .
. . . .

In what ways has becoming a Christ follower changed your future plans?
. . . .
. . . .
. . . .
. . . .

Write about a time when you felt God wanted to lead you away from something you enjoyed. . . . .
. . . .
. . . .
. . . .
. . . .
. . . .
. . . .

Why do you think He wanted you to give that thing up? . . . .
. . . .
. . . .
. . . .

How long did you fight Him? . . . .
. . . .

How did you feel during the process? . . . .
. . . .

What happened in your heart when you finally gave that dream over to God?
. . . .
. . . .

How has He rewarded your obedience? . . . .
. . . .
. . . .
. . . .

joy

Read Matthew 4:18-22 and 9:9.

What did Jesus' disciples give up in order to follow Him?

. . . .

. . . .

. . . .

How do you think their families and friends reacted? . . . .

. . . .

. . . .

. . . .

. . . .

List at least three ways God blessed their huge sacrifice. . . . .

. . . .

. . . .

. . . .

. . . .

Put yourself in the place of one of these disciples. Write a letter or journal entry
that he might have written at the end of his life, regarding his life-altering change of
plans. . . . .

. . . .

. . . .

. . . .

. . . .

. . . .

. . . .

. . . .

. . . .

Where I Belong

it was nice to see him

I was studying a very boring California history book, when the doorbell rang. I tossed my book aside and ran to see who was there. I expected to see one of my sister's friends, or a neighbor needing to borrow an egg from Mom. Instead, it was a face from the past.

"Hey, Robert." I hugged him. We hadn't seen each other since high school graduation, a few months earlier. We'd been on the speech team together, shared a couple of the same classes, and gone out on one "group date" as friends. We'd never been close friends, but still, it was nice to see him.

Robert stepped inside. "I was across the street and just thought I'd stop by and say, 'Hi.'"

We talked for a while about what we had been up to since graduation, the college classes that we liked and hated. Finally Robert said, "Well, I have to get home. I have Bible study tonight."

I hadn't even known he was a Christian. "Where do you go to church?"

I envied Robert when he told me about his church and its great college group. My family hadn't been to church in almost two years. Mom had had some health problems, so Sunday morning services slipped to the bottom of the priority list. She was better now, but we hadn't returned to church yet.

I must admit, at first I didn't mind sleeping in on Sunday mornings, skipping sermons and lectures from the youth group leader. I figured I could read my Bible on my own. And hey, I didn't need to go to church to be a Christian, right? But whenever I ran into someone from our old congregation who said, "We've missed you. Is your family attending another church now?"

I found myself making excuses. More and more often, when I woke up late on a Sunday morning I thought, This feels wrong. We should be at church like other Christian families.

"What about you?" Robert asked. "What church do you go to?"

Cringing with guilt, I gave him my standard half-truth answer. "We're kind of between churches right now."

"Well, do you want to go with me tonight? I can pick you up."

My heart felt like it was almost jumping up and down, screaming, "Please say 'Yes.' Please, please!"

"That would be great," I said, more calmly than my insides would have liked.

"Then I'll be back here at about quarter to seven."

I raced through the rest of my history chapter, ate a quick dinner, and searched for my Bible. When was the last time that I felt so excited about a church activity?

Later that evening, I sat with Robert in a large fellowship hall, trying to pick up on the words to new worship songs. I was so relieved when the song leaders chose one that I remembered from my old youth group.

past

team

great

excuses

wrong

past

team

great

excuses

wrong

Really though, the music didn't matter. I overflowed with a happiness that comes only from fellowship with God's people. For the first time in ages, I was where I needed to be—in a room full of young men and women who loved God and wanted to learn more about Him. I'd already decided that, if Robert didn't invite me to join him again on Sunday morning, I would be bold and invite myself. I had a lot of catching up to do in my walk with God, and I couldn't wait to get started.

I couldn't stop thanking God for sending Robert to my door that day. Through him, I found a new church home and a great group of Christians who I immediately felt comfortable with— something I had never really had, even in the church we attended for years before Mom got sick. More importantly, I understood the power of being part of a spiritual family. No wonder the Bible warns us not to neglect public worship. Our souls need it.

Sure, I could read my Bible at home. Skipping Sunday morning services had not erased my salvation. But had I grown? Not at all. If anything, I'd lost spiritual muscle. Was I content? No. The guilt, isolation from fellow-believers, and the lack of heavenly nourishment had left me empty and miserable—until now.

Thank You for bringing me back, God, I prayed as we prepared to break up into small groups. Don't ever let me forget how great this feels! And please don't let me wander away again.

a special prayer

Thank You God, for the privilege that I have, to learn and worship openly with other believers. Forgive me for the times when I let other things get in the way. Fill me with a desire to learn more about You, not just on Sunday mornings, but each day. Amen.

questions:

For me, going to church is:
❑ Part of life
❑ A highlight of my week
❑ Boring
❑ Something that I wish my family would do more often

If you checked the second or third choices, explain why. . . . .
. . . .
. . . .
. . . .

Think back to the last time that you went through a major struggle. Did you have a group of Christians around to help you through it? How did they help? If you were not attending church at the time, how might things have turned out differently, if you'd had that support? . . . .
. . . .
. . . .
. . . .

Think of someone you know who has either stopped showing up on Sunday mornings or doesn't see public worship as important. Does she seem to have genuine joy? . . . .

Pray for this friend and ask God to draw her to a church home.

joy

dig deeper

Hebrews 10:19-25 addresses the importance of not neglecting public worship. Think about times when you neglected church and/or youth group attendance. What kept you away? . . . .

. . . .

. . . .

. . . .

How did you feel about it? . . . .

. . . .

. . . .

What effect did it have on your spiritual growth and relationship with God?

. . . .

. . . .

How does church and youth group attendance affect your attitude, choices, and moods? . . . .

. . . .

. . . .

. . . .

Acts 2:42-47 shows the early church at its best. In what ways does your church family reflect the early church's spirit of generosity, fellowship, Christ-like love, and devotion to biblical teaching? . . . .

. . . .

. . . .

. . . .

. . . .

. . . .

. . . .

FOCUS ON THE FAMILY®

teen outreach

At Focus on the Family, we work to help you really get to know Jesus and equip you to change your world for Him.

We realize the struggles you face are different from your parents' or your little brother's, so we've developed a lot of resources specifically to help you live boldly for Christ, no matter what's happening in your life.

Besides teen events and a live call-in show, we have Web sites, magazines, booklets, devotionals and novels...all dealing with the stuff you care about. For a detailed listing of the latest resources, log on to our Web site at **go.family.org/teens.**

Focus on the Family Magazines

We know you want to stay up-to-date on the latest in your world—but it's hard to find information on relationships, entertainment, trends and teen issues that doesn't drag you down. It's even harder to find magazines that deliver what you want and need from a Christ-honoring perspective.

That's why we created *Breakaway*® (for teen guys), *Brio*® (for teen girls 12 to 16), *Brio & Beyond*® (for girls ages 16 and up). So, don't be left out—sign up today!

Breakaway®
Teen guys
www.breakawaymag.com

Brio®
Teen girls 13 to 15
www.briomag.com

Brio & Beyond®
Teen girls 16 to 19
www.briomag.com

Teen Talk Radio
www.lifeontheedgelive.com

Phone toll free: (800) A-FAMILY (232-6459)

In Canada, log on to www.focusonthefamily.ca

In Canada, call toll free: (800) 661-9800

want more?

Want More?™ Life

Go from ordinary to extraordinary! *Want More? Life* will help teen girls open the door to God's abundant life. They'll go deeper, wider, and higher in their walks with God in the midst of everyday challenges like self-image, guys, godly friendships, and big decisions.

Want More?™ Love

Teen girls may ask, "Does God really love me? How can He love me — with all my faults and flaws?" *Want More? Love* is a powerful devotional that shows girls how passionately and protectively God loves and cares for them — and how they can love Him in return! Get the first book, *Want More? Life*, too!

Brio Girls® Series

Real faith meets real life in these popular novels that give teen girls a glimpse of reality and its consequences. Girls identify with the characters as they make decisions about school and boys and learn how to manage relationships.

Look for these special books in your Christian bookstore. To request a copy, call (800) A-FAMILY (232-6459) or log on to http://go.family.org/teens or write to Focus on the Family Colorado Springs, CO 80995.
Friends in Canada may write to Focus on the Family,
PO Box 9800, Stn Terminal, Vancouver, BC V6B 4G3 or call (800) 661-9800.

Visit our Web site (www.family.org) to learn more about the ministry or find out if there is a Focus on the Family office in your country.

THREE RESOURCES TO STRENGTHEN YOUR FAITH

Stand

Are you ready to know what you believe — and why you believe it? Once you know what you believe — and why you believe it — you'll be ready to bring the light of Christ into the dark strongholds of our world . . . and stand forever!

Airborne

If your faith journey feels more like a crawl through the dust, it's time for you to catch some air! Amazing stories from popular youth evangelist Jose Zayas' own life, plus dynamic truths from the Word of God make *Airborne* a must-have for new teen followers of Christ as well as those of you still searching for truth.

Bloom

Teen girls have lots of questions about life. In *Bloom: A Girl's Guide To Growing Up*, their questions are addressed and answered with the straightforward honesty teens expect and demand. From changing bodies, to dating and sex, to relationships, money, and more, girls will find the answers they need.

Look for these special books in your Christian bookstore. To request a copy, call (800) A-FAMILY (232-6459) or log on to http://go.family.org/teens or write to Focus on the Family Colorado Springs, CO 80995.
Friends in Canada may write to Focus on the Family,
PO Box 9800, Stn Terminal, Vancouver, BC V6B 4G3 or call (800) 661-9800.

Visit our Web site (www.family.org) to learn more about the ministry or find out if there is a Focus on the Family office in your country.